"I have a very simple business proposition for you, Mr. Salvatore."

Penelope fixed Stefano Salvatore with her most determined gaze, and continued, "I want you to marry me."

If she'd startled him, he didn't show it by so much as a flicker of expression. "Since when did marriage become a business proposition?" he asked.

"Marriage is always a business proposition."

He surprised her with a quick, flashing smile. He was extraordinarily good-looking. "I see. Thank you, Ms...?"

"Wentworth. Penelope Wentworth."

A hint of amusement drifted through his gaze. "Thank you, Ms. Wentworth. But I'm not interested in marriage."

Day Leclaire and her family live in the midst of a maritime forest on a small island off the coast of North Carolina. Despite the yearly storms that batter them and the frequent power outages, they find the beautiful climate, superb fishing and unbeatable seascape more than adequate compensation. One of their first acquisitions upon moving to Hatteras Island was a cat named Fuzzy. He has recently discovered that laps are wonderful places to curl up and nap—and that Day's son really was kidding when he named the hamster Cat Food.

THE BRIDE'S PROPOSITION
Day Leclaire

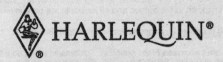

TORONTO • NEW YORK • LONDON
AMSTERDAM • PARIS • SYDNEY • HAMBURG
STOCKHOLM • ATHENS • TOKYO • MILAN • MADRID
PRAGUE • WARSAW • BUDAPEST • AUCKLAND

To an extraordinary editor, Samantha Bell,
with my deepest thanks and gratitude.

ISBN 0-373-03611-6

THE BRIDE'S PROPOSITION

First North American Publication 2000.

PROLOGUE

"STEFANO SALVATORE is the absolute, hands-down, last man on this earth I'd ever trust."

"Oh, come now. Why do you say that?"

Penelope leaned across the tiny table where she sat, ostensibly to reach for a pitcher of cream for her coffee. In truth, she was blatantly eavesdropping on the conversation going on beside her and didn't want to miss a single word. The two chatting women were both young and attractive, clearly businesswomen taking advantage of the warm, sunny weather to lunch at an open-air café that catered to the suit-and-tie crowd in downtown San Francisco.

They were also talking about the very man Penelope intended to proposition.

"Granted, they weren't able to prove anything," said the first woman, a perky blonde who radiated shrewd intelligence. "But everyone knows he did it, Lisa. The facts are indisputable."

The second woman—Lisa—nodded. "A logical deduction supported by circumstantial, if not direct evidence. How...unfortunate." She was a brunette-haired beauty with pouty lips highlighted an interesting shade of plum and the sort of sultry voice that left men puddled on the floor. "Such a shame when a good man falls from grace. Honor is so rare these days."

The blonde shook her head. "I doubt anyone will ever trust him again. Not on a business front, even with the Salvatore name behind him. And no woman in her right mind would trust him as a lover. Not after what he did to his ex-fiancée.''

"But, Kim, I've heard he's so good-looking."

"Oh, he's gorgeous. That just makes him all the more dangerous. Women adore him. Or they did. He excels at smooth charm and Mediterranean graciousness. One of those men who makes you feel you're the most adored creature on earth. You know the sort I mean?''

Lisa released a half moan, half sigh and Penelope ducked her head to hide a smile. The irony was almost too much. Here she sat, an investigative dossier on Stefano Salvatore open in front of her, and she was learning more about the man in a few minutes of crass eavesdropping than what she'd read in the first twenty pages of the report. If only she'd had the opportunity to get to know Kim before this, she could have saved herself a fortune in detective's fees.

"Maybe the rumors are wrong," the brunette offered. "I mean, you said yourself that nobody could prove anything.''

"Nor did he defend himself. And Kate Bennett, his fiancée, left him when the story broke. Come on. Use your common sense. Since she was the one most intimately affected, she must have known the truth about the incident.''

"Where there's smoke?" Lisa asked delicately.

"There's not just a fire, but an inferno. If he'd been innocent, don't you think she'd have stuck by him?''

"I assume by leaving she pretty much confirmed his guilt?''

"Oh, he's guilty." Kim hammered home her point by rapping a French manicured fingernail against the tabletop. "I doubt he'll ever be able to repair his reputation despite all the Salvatore brothers rallying around him.

You watch at tonight's charity benefit. Assuming Stefano has the nerve to show up, people will keep a careful distance. No one will want to be associated with him. Who'd want to risk being seen doing business with a thief?''

Lisa grinned. ''Or be caught in bed with one?''

Kim glanced around and Penelope made a production of studying her file so she wouldn't be caught staring. ''To tell the truth, it's tempting. If I weren't afraid of losing my job, I just might be willing to chance it.''

''He's that attractive?''

''Looks like a dark angel and acts like one, too.''

''I'm drooling.''

''You'd do more than drool if you saw him.'' Kim checked her watch. ''Come on. It's getting late and I still have that Carter deal to put together before the end of the day. Will you be at the benefit tonight?''

''After the buildup you've given Salvatore? I wouldn't miss it!''

''Then I'll see you there.''

Penelope waited until the two women left the café before gathering the file spread before her. The conversation she'd overheard put the final touches on the information her detective had gathered and she smiled in satisfaction. It also allowed her to reach a decision.

Stefano Salvatore was perfect. He was everything she hoped and more. Of course, it was the ''more'' that had her a little concerned. But no matter. She'd find a way around that part. Anchoring several bills beneath her coffee cup, Penelope left the restaurant and walked briskly toward Salvatores. She wouldn't delay this matter any further. Time to speak directly to Stefano. Time to make him a small—and she hoped irresistible—business proposition.

Time to be caught in bed with the man.

CHAPTER ONE

"I HAVE a very simple business proposition for you, Mr. Salvatore." Penelope Wentworth made herself comfortable in the chair across from her chosen target and adjusted a pair of practical wire-rimmed glasses before fixing Stefano with her most determined gaze. It could be quite determined, too, considering she'd been using it to great effect since the tender age of ten. "I want you to marry me."

If she'd startled him, he didn't show it by so much as a flicker of expression. Instead he kept his dark brown eyes trained on her as though she were a unique specimen he'd never seen before. She was used to that, too, often finding herself on the receiving end of that type of look—also since the tender age of ten. The looks didn't bother her. At least they hadn't since she'd turned twelve and learned that the adults in her world were far more intimidated by her than she was by them.

"Since when did marriage become a business proposition?" he asked.

She almost smiled at the casual way he asked the question, as though he were indulging idle curiosity. She might have believed him if it weren't for the deadly stillness that had seized him the instant she'd popped her question. "Marriage is always a business proposition. Most people cover up that fact by hiding behind an excess of emotion. A foolish indulgence, if you ask me."

He surprised her with a quick, flashing smile and she forced herself to conceal her reaction, though it was dif-

ficult. She should have given more credence to Kim's
claim about him, instead of dismissing it as the sort of
feminine exaggeration women indulged in when attracted to a man. Kim hadn't exaggerated. Not even a
little. It annoyed Penelope to discover that all the re-
search and computations she'd run on Stefano Salvatore
had failed to take into consideration the sheer presence
of the man. It was quite a presence. "Dark angel" struck
her as all too apt.

He was extraordinarily good-looking, his features arranged in a way guaranteed to turn most women into
total idiots. And yet, he still managed to retain an air of
undeniable masculinity. His arching cheekbones tempted
a woman's touch, while an aggressive nose kept him
from appearing too pretty. A bold, kissable mouth sat at
odds with his square, authoritative—and no doubt, stubborn—jawline. Thick black hair tumbled across his brow
above the most enticing earthy brown eyes she'd ever
seen. Calm. Knowing. Focused. And sharply intelligent.

"I see. Thank you, Ms....?"

"Wentworth. Penelope Wentworth."

A hint of amusement drifted through his gaze—a gaze
almost as disconcerting as her own. "Thank you, Ms.
Wentworth. But I'm not interested in marriage, whether
it's a business proposition, a romantic entanglement or
at the end of a shotgun."

"I see," she said with a brisk nod. "I assume that's
a direct result of your failed engagement and that unfortunate incident that preceded it."

He surged to his feet and Penelope pressed her spine
tight against the back of her chair. Oh, dear. Maybe she
should have chosen a different angle. This had clearly
been the wrong one with which to initiate negotiations.
He circled his desk with slow, deliberate strides, coming

to halt directly beside her chair. When he reached for her, it took every ounce of self-possession not to flinch. Not that her well-practiced self-possession helped. Grasping her arms, he yanked her from the chair and towed her toward the door to his office, her glasses bouncing on the tip of her nose with every step.

"What are you doing?" she demanded. My goodness! She sounded downright breathless. That had never happened before.

"I'm throwing you out of my office, Ms. Wentworth."

"Would you mind telling me why?"

"I don't mind in the least." He wrapped a large hand around the knob and yanked open the door. "I don't marry nutcases. Hell, Nellie. I don't even talk to them." With that, he propelled her from his office and slammed the door in her face.

Well! Penelope frowned at the solid oak door as she straightened her glasses. How rude. He hadn't even listened to what she had to say. Not giving herself time to reconsider, she turned the knob and reentered the room. He must not have been accustomed to having people cross him. He'd returned to his desk and buried himself in his work. It wasn't until she slammed the door that he looked up.

She caught her breath at the expression in his eyes. Why had she thought they were calm? They were the most volatile and impassioned she'd ever seen. Slowly he regained his feet, thrusting back his chair with such force, it crashed against the wall behind him, making the windows shimmer.

"What part of being thrown out don't you understand?"

A trace of a lilting accent slipped into his words, adding a raw, elemental quality to his anger. She lifted her chin and poked her wire-rimmed glasses more firmly on the bridge of her nose. If he thought he could intimidate her, he'd have to work a lot harder than glaring and tossing chairs around and smoldering with overwrought testosterone. She'd faced endless business meetings with an endless assortment of testosterone-wrought males. She could handle one more. After all, it was simple emotion and simple emotion rarely withstood the overpowering force of cool, calculated logic.

Besides... She was determined.

"Mr. Salvatore, you haven't bothered to hear my proposition."

"And I don't intend to."

Italian. Definitely an Italian accent. Why did it have to be something so darned sexy? Not that she'd allow sex to sway her. Much. "What if it involves Janus Corporation?" she asked, forcibly restricting her focus to the business at hand.

She'd gotten him with that one. He folded his impressive arms across an equally impressive chest. "Go on."

Gesturing toward the chair, she offered her most engaging smile. "You were going to invite me to have a seat, I believe."

The smile worked. It often did, perhaps because it was wide and nonthreatening. Or perhaps because it was a bit lopsided. Whatever the appeal, a hint of amusement glittered in his eyes again. Penelope had learned long ago to use whatever tools worked best in business. Sure, a woman should be logical in her dealings. Still, a certain amount of plain friendliness didn't hurt. It was personal involvement that she fought to avoid. Because personal involvement led to illogical business decisions, something to be avoided at all costs. She'd learned that lesson years ago and she didn't intend to ever forget it.

Stefano pointed a finger at the chair she'd vacated. "Please. Sit," he ordered in a tone that had her clamping her teeth together in silent protest.

A thousand inappropriate retorts tempted her, but she bit back every single one. Shooting off her mouth without thinking was one of her most serious failings, something she couldn't afford to indulge at this particular juncture. Besides, the chair in front of his desk was precisely where she wanted to be, even if the invitation to occupy it had sounded suspiciously like a command. *Let's be honest,* she silently scolded. If she didn't have a nasty tendency to take charge in any given situation, she wouldn't have found his "request" quite so irritating.

Determined to be gracious, she sat. "You're too kind," she murmured, hoping he didn't catch the dry tone.

If he did, he ignored it. "What's your interest in Janus Corporation and why would that tempt me into a marriage with you?"

"You certainly get right to the point, don't you? I like that," she approved. "None of that false charm you Salvatore men pride yourself on."

"You don't find me charming?" he asked a bit too politely.

A trace of an accent rippled through his voice again, brushing her with the faint warmth of distant Mediterranean climes. It was a dead giveaway. The man was in a mild temper. It would seem that emotion brought out the most elemental part of Mr. Salvatore's personality. Penelope smiled, filing the information away for future reference. Perhaps she could make that work to her advantage at some point.

"No, I don't find you the least charming," she lied with aplomb. Not that it would be a lie for long. All she needed was a little time and effort to eradicate any such foolish inclination. Charm suggested a quality outside of business, and right now she didn't have room in her life for anything that fell outside the realm of business.

"Excellent. I've recently discovered that charm is a mistake when it comes to women."

She hesitated, considering that for a moment. Did he really mean all women or just her? A surge of something uncomfortably soft and feminine stirred to life. What would happen if Stefano changed his mind and concentrated the full force of his personality on her? She'd caught a brief flash of his smile—a smile that would prove quite dangerous for a less sensible woman. She'd also been forced to acknowledge his masculine good looks coupled with an equally masculine strength. In the past, she'd always been prudent enough to keep that male energy at a safe distance. How would she handle being married to it?

Darn it! It boiled down to sheer male presence again, which had to be a deliberate ploy on his part. Why else would she be experiencing these ridiculous impulses? She'd have to reconfigure her calculations to include that annoying element. Perhaps Stefano Salvatore wasn't her best choice, after all. He struck her as far too aggressive and entirely too independent. Somehow she doubted he'd take instruction well, particularly from a temporary wife.

Then the flaw in her reasoning dawned on her and she rewarded him with a broad, approving smile. His comments weren't aimed at her. He truly did mean *all* women. It was an attitude, she suspected, brought on by his broken engagement—along with that rather unfortunate incident involving his fiancée's family business. The combination of those two factors must have had a profound effect on him. Penelope kept a perfectly natural twinge of sympathy hidden, suspecting he wouldn't appreciate it in the least.

"We're back to that unmentionable topic, aren't we?" she dared to ask.

"So it would seem."

"Then charm is out." She didn't phrase it as a question.

He nodded. "Which leaves us with business. Shall we get to it?"

"I assume my choices are to say 'yes' to that question or get ousted?" she hazarded a guess.

"Smart woman. Now who are you, what do you want and what do you have to do with Janus Corporation?"

"I own it," she explained simply.

"The company is owned by Crabbe and Associates."

She grimaced. "Terrible name, isn't it?"

"Dreadful."

His sarcasm didn't escape her notice and she released her breath in a long sigh. "All right, Mr. Salvatore. I won't waste any more of your precious time, since I prefer to stay focused on the business at hand, as well. I *am* Crabbe and Associates, just as I *am* Janus Corporation. They all belong to me."

"I assume you have some sort of proof."

"I could provide it without too much difficulty."

He took a moment to digest that. To her surprise he didn't shove the phone in her direction or insist on her handing over irrefutable evidence then and there. Instead he concentrated his shrewd gaze on her for endless moments. "How old are you?" he asked at last.

For some reason the question struck her as amusing. "What does that have to do with anything?"

"I'm curious."

"I'm twenty-six."

"Rather young to be in such a position of power."

"Oh, I'm not in the main position of power. I just own the two companies. My uncle runs them."

"And that annoys you? Do you feel you should be in charge?"

She stared blankly. "Feelings have nothing to do with my decision." They'd gotten off track and she attempted to steer them back in the appropriate direction. "Mr. Salvatore—"

"Stefano."

She inclined her head. After all, if they were to be married, it would be ludicrous to insist on calling him by his last name. "Stefano. Are you interested in purchasing Janus Corporation?"

"My family's been trying to buy that company for years now. It would give Salvatores a lock on the West Coast market."

"Well, I'm in a position to see that your family gets its wish."

"And all it's going to cost me is marriage to you?"

"Exactly."

"Why?"

She left the chair with less than her usual care. To her distress, she found this an emotional issue, one she had difficulty articulating. How would a man like Stefano Salvatore understand what she'd come to realize was vital to her future...not to mention her uncle's?

"If you marry me, I'll sell you Janus Corporation at a rock-bottom price."

"Once again... *Why?*"

"Because marriage is the only way I'll receive full possession of my inheritance." She wandered through his sitting area, running her hand over a large, cushy couch and matching chair. The colors appealed, the warm earth tones accented by splashes of invigorating jewel colors. Realizing Stefano was patiently waiting for her to continue, she faced him from behind the comforting buffer of the furniture. "Until I'm either forty or married, my assets remain in my uncle's control."

"So you want my help in staging a coup." His accent was back, a bit heavier this time and edgy with emotion. "At the great age of twenty-six, you've decided you can do a better job than your uncle, is that it?"

She chuckled, a ridiculously deep, rumbling sound that would have been better suited to a large, bass-voiced man. It invariably provoked delighted laughter in response. But aside from a betraying twitch of his lips, Stefano remained silent. "No, I don't think I can do better than my uncle. Loren is an excellent businessman. In the years he's been managing my inheritance, it's grown tenfold."

"Then why are you so anxious to take over?"

She couldn't tell him that—at least, not the true reason. It would be inappropriate and quite likely unethical. She wandered to another section of his office, this one displaying a grouping of photographs. They were all family pictures and envy filled her. It would seem the Salvatores were as prolific as they were handsome. There were at least a half dozen men in a variety of shots, varying in age from their mid-twenties to mid-thirties. She scanned them swiftly. Stefano—dangerously charming smile in place—popped out at her from all the photos, far too many images for her own peace of mind.

Penelope picked up one of the portraits and examined it. Oh, dear. Her vision was definitely playing tricks on her. She could swear that more than one Stefano grinned up at her. The odd warmth she'd experienced earlier returned with stunning impact. She wasn't interested in him as a man, she tried to tell herself. And yet... What other explanation could there be for her peculiar reaction? She returned the frame to its former position with awkward haste. The metal frame clattered against the wooden table and she backed cautiously away. This was neither the time nor place for sexual attraction. To have it crop up with Stefano was as annoying as it was inconvenient.

"You still haven't answered my question," he prompted.

She cleared her throat. "I know."

"Is it such a difficult one?"

Taking a deep breath, she turned. He stood far too near. Thank goodness he wasn't destroying her concentration with a smile, though the intentness of those rich brown eyes disturbed her almost as much. He'd also doused himself with a delicious cologne. Well... Perhaps "doused" overstated the fact considering how the light, spicy fragrance only teased her senses when he came uncomfortably close. If she wanted to complain about anything it should be about the height and breadth of him looming over her. Even covered by the civilized trappings of a business suit she could detect the subtle ridging along his shoulders and chest, warning of the hard muscular frame beneath. And this unsettling—not to mention gorgeous—example of manhood was the one she'd selected to marry. She almost groaned aloud.

How disastrous.

"Sometimes I have trouble putting all my cards on the table," she confessed, shifting to give herself a bit more room.

He blocked her with a graceful twist of his body. "Try."

"Okay."

She eased past him and crossed to a large picture window overlooking the city of San Francisco. Ironically his office building faced her own, only the width of a city street separating them. He followed, crowding close once again, and she glanced over her shoulder in exasperation. Did this man have *no* sense of personal distance? Apparently not.

"My father owned Crabbe & Associates. He was the one who built it up from a tiny firm to a rather impressive corporation. My uncle was his right-hand man. When my parents were killed in a small plane crash, Uncle Loren took over both me and the business."

"How old were you?"

"Ten."

"But you said he's a good businessman?"

"Oh, he excels at it."

"Was he also a good parent?"

She smiled at the hint of concern in Stefano's voice. Despite his hardness, a strong protective streak ran wide and deep through the man. She suspected it came from being part of such a large family. Having so many siblings to look after could account for his attitude toward her. "Uncle Loren's a bit gruff and was rather bewildered by everything involved in raising a little girl. But he loves me."

"Then what's the problem?"

"When my uncle took me in, he decided that I should learn about my inheritance and how Crabbe and Associates operated. So I began attending a few select board meetings."

It didn't surprise Stefano that she'd dodged his question, despite her apparent directness. In the short time he'd known her, he'd discovered the delectable Ms. Wentworth didn't like discussing personal matters. Tough. She'd forced herself on him with her insane marriage proposal. That opened the door to any damn question he cared to ask. "Did you enjoy the meetings?"

Her expression reflected sheer bliss, her entire body vibrating with the strength of her enthusiasm. "Yes, I did, much to my uncle's delight. It gave us something in common. As the years went by, I became more and more involved. I have a degree in business and international finance and have an active position on the board of both Crabbe and Associates and Janus Corp."

He frowned. "I still don't—"

"I've lived and breathed the corporate world for sixteen years now. That's long enough to know what I want from the businesses I own." Drifting from the window to his bookcase, she plucked free a heavy volume and flipped through it without any real interest. He suspected she was using it as an excuse not to look at him. Interesting. "It's time to point Crabbe and Associates in a new direction."

"So you *are* intent on taking control away from your uncle." An inexplicable disappointment gripped him. "What makes you think I'd help?"

She slammed the book closed and returned it to the shelf before facing him. She had the most unusual golden eyes he'd ever seen, as penetrating as they were disconcerting, a thick sweep of brown lashes adding to their allure. "Because you want Janus."

"There's a lot of things I want in this world, Nellie." His voice hardened. "That doesn't mean I take them regardless of the consequences. Or did you think that 'unfortunate incident' as you phrased it earlier, might make me more susceptible to your offer?"

She shot him another of the wide, appealing smiles he'd found so attractive. "The thought crossed my mind, although not for the reason you might think. I'm not propositioning you because I think you're unethical and therefore likely to go along with my plan. I'm propositioning you because this is the perfect opportunity to prove everyone wrong. To prove that you're an honorable man."

Harsh lines scored his face. "You're so sure I am? Or is it that you haven't heard the stories?"

"I've heard the stories."

"Then what the *hell* are you doing here?"

"I don't believe them," she replied with breathtaking simplicity.

For a moment he could only stare. The air burned in his lungs, fighting for release. He exhaled roughly. "You don't—"

"No."

Suspicion was quick to override an irrational surge of hope—a hope he'd thought ripped from him long ago. "And how did you arrive at that brilliant deduction?"

"I had you investigated."

"If you had me investigated then how can you believe I'm—"

She waved him silent with an imperious sweep of her hand. He let her get away with it. This time. "It doesn't take much analysis. The whole matter is quite logical.

You were engaged to a Kate Bennett. Her family owned a small, but profitable company interested in picking up a lucrative contract with an overseas corporation. You played middleman, putting the deal together. Unfortunately the overseas corporation proved to be fraudulent, nothing more than a paper front.''

"You're not telling me anything I don't already know," he interrupted. "I lived it, remember?''

She fixed him with an impassive stare, one Stefano suspected she'd cultivated over the course of her business career. No doubt it worked on most men. Unfortunately for her, he wasn't most men. "I'm recapping the points to put the entire story in perspective.''

"Sorry." His tone warned he was anything but. "Do continue.''

"Where was I? Oh, yes. As a result of the scam, Ms. Bennett's family lost their collective shirts. Salvatores reimbursed the money the Bennetts lost, but it was too late. The damage had already been done. Though nothing could be proven, rumor cast you as the villain of the piece. The appearance of impropriety, you understand.'' She added the last comment with impressive delicacy. "In my opinion, that appearance was exacerbated when Ms. Bennett called off the engagement and Salvatores paid back the monies that were lost.''

"I understand all about the appearance of impropriety.''

"A shame really," she reflected, as though he hadn't spoken. "Since you weren't the guilty party.''

"Once again, Ms. Wentworth... How would you know that? We used all of our contacts to try to uncover who was behind that dummy overseas company. We came up empty. What information did you uncover that we've been unable to?''

"None."

An irrational anger gripped him. "Then how can you believe I'm innocent?"

"Because it doesn't make sense," she replied with a calm assurance that amazed him. No one other than his family had ever supported him with such absolute, blanket certainty. "There's no reason for you to cheat the Bennetts. In fact, you went out of your way to help them. Your engagement predated the business arrangement, therefore you didn't seduce her in order to buy her silence. You also aren't in financial difficulties. There was no overt need for you to steal. Not that people steal just for need. But as far as I've been able to determine, there's no underlying factor that would motivate your actions. To suddenly start stealing at this juncture doesn't make sense."

"Your investigator told you all that?"

"Some of it."

"And as a result of his analysis, he decided I wasn't guilty?"

She adjusted her glasses, the intensity of her huge golden eyes enhanced by the lenses. "Quite the contrary. He assumed you were guilty, the same as all the others. But he was wrong." She made a face. "I'm afraid he's not terribly logical."

"Are you telling me that even though we've never met, even though all the evidence is stacked against me, even though your own investigator agrees with the general consensus as to my guilt...you don't?"

Her lopsided smile flickered to life. "Exactly."

"You don't seem to understand." He kept every scrap of emotion from his voice. "No one believes me except my family. Not friends who've known me all my life.

Not business associates I've worked with for years. Not
my former fiancée nor her family. No one."

"I do."

He stared at her in utter disbelief. Her brilliant gaze
held his, the sincerity in her eyes forcing him to realize
the truth. *She believed him.* "You're serious."

"Dead serious. And if you marry me, I'm hoping
we'll have an opportunity to prove it."

"How?"

A small frown eclipsed her smile. "To be honest, I'm
not sure. I thought we could work that out between us
at a later date. Of course, marriage to me will help.
Believe it or not, people trust me. If I say you're trust-
worthy, few will stand up and question my judgment."

"And why's that?"

She shrugged modestly. "Because I'm usually right.
To be honest, I can't remember the last time I wasn't."

"But, what if you're wrong?" He couldn't explain
what drove him to ask the question. Still, he had to
know. "What if I *am* a thief? What if you simply haven't
discovered my particular motivating force?"

Her deep laughter reached out to enclose him, her
fine-boned stature at odds with the lush, full-bodied
sound. The incongruity fascinated him. "I'll certainly
look foolish, won't I? But I doubt that will happen. I
trust my analytical skills and ability to formulate logical
deductions."

"Very intimidating," he said dryly.

She grinned. "But you're not intimidated, are you?"

"Not even a little." He thrust a hand through his hair.
"This is crazy."

"I've caught you by surprise," she sympathized.
"I'm afraid it couldn't be helped. I want to keep my
proposition quiet."

His eyes narrowed. "You still haven't told me why you've decided you should have control of Crabbe."

For the first time since she'd walked into his office, her expression closed over. It made him realize just how open she'd been with him until that point. "I'm sorry, but I can't answer that question. There's more to the story than I can explain at this juncture."

"Why doesn't that surprise me?"

She tilted her head to one side, the light catching in the strands of her dark blond hair and highlighting the scattered threads of gold. "Should I assume your disapproval means you won't marry me?"

"Of course I'm not going to marry you," he snapped. "Salvatores only marry for—"

"Love?"

Her voice had acquired far too gentle a tone, her keen gaze revealing entirely too much sympathy. *"Non ne posso più!"* In fact, he'd had more than enough. "I no longer believe in that particular myth."

"Then I don't understand the problem."

He fought to control his temper, a fierce impatience straining it to the limits. "One near miss does not encourage me to make another."

"I'm not asking for a permanent relationship, you understand."

"And I'm supposed to find that more attractive? A failed engagement followed by a failed marriage? That would sit well with my family. And it will do wonders for my reputation in the business community."

"Oh, dear. I didn't think of that." Dismay bronzed the gold of her eyes. "I see your problem."

"Good. Now let me counter your offer. Once you marry, drop by for a visit. I'd be happy to divest you of Janus Corporation."

"What if that's the corporation my husband wants in exchange for marrying me?"

"Is that likely?"

She hesitated, catching a lush lip between her teeth. "Didn't I mention?"

He released his breath in an impatient sigh. "Mention what?"

"The next name on my list is your chief competitor."

CHAPTER TWO

STEFANO fought back a groan. Aw, hell. "Tell me you're not talking about Cornell."

"If you mean Robert Cornell of Cornell Industries, International, then yes." Apparently Penelope Wentworth didn't see the need to pull her punches. "He's also single, in case you didn't know."

Stefano gritted his teeth. "No, I didn't."

"If it makes you feel any better, you're my first choice."

"Lucky me."

"As you know, if you owned Janus Corporation you'd have the majority interest along the West Coast." She pressed home her point. "Your import/export firm would be unrivaled."

"Salvatore's is a little more than an import/export business."

She nodded impatiently. "I understand that you specialize in procurement of goods and services. As I mentioned, I had your company thoroughly investigated. The bottom line is this—you either acquire Janus or Cornell does. If Cornell gets it..." She shrugged. "I don't have to tell you what that would mean."

"I'm well aware that your actions would have severe consequences on my family's business."

"I'd think that would make your decision all the easier." Her smile turned mischievous. "Don't you think I'm the lesser of two evils?"

He almost laughed, despite his predicament. "I think that sums it up perfectly."

Her rumbling chuckle teased his senses again, at odds with her businesslike attitude. "Let me mention a few final details." She ticked off on her finger. "I won't inflict myself on you for long, I promise. And I wouldn't expect you to consummate the relationship. Nor do I plan to make any marital demands on your time. Does that help at all?"

"And if *I* decided to make demands?"

To his surprise, she didn't hesitate. "The marriage could be on any terms that work best for you. I have a goal to meet. If that involves some sort of sacrifice on my part, so be it."

"Very magnanimous."

The dryness of his tone must have penetrated. She took a deep breath and nodded briskly. Stefano had witnessed enough Salvatore board meetings to determine their negotiations had just ended. He could read the decision in her expression and in the determined carriage of her body. His mouth tugged to one side. In the little time he'd known her he'd discovered that Ms. Penelope Wentworth was nothing if not determined. Apparently, when she wanted something, she went after it with unwavering tenacity. She approached, holding out her hand. He took it in his, sensing the strength beneath the softness.

"You have twenty-four hours, should you change your mind. I'm hoping to schedule an appointment with Mr. Cornell for noon tomorrow."

"You're serious about this? You'll marry a man you don't know? Get rid of one of your companies just so you can control your inheritance?"

"I'm quite serious."

"And there isn't any way I can convince you to sell Janus Corporation?"

"Not without marriage." Regret edged her voice. "It isn't within my power, remember? Not while Uncle Loren controls everything."

She didn't delay. Crossing to the door, she left without a backward glance. The instant she'd gone, Stefano snatched up the phone and punched in a series of numbers. "It's Salvatore. I have a job for you." He frowned at the door. "I want all the information you can dig up on a woman named Penelope Wentworth. And I want it yesterday."

He dropped the receiver into the cradle and crossed to the window. If he wasn't mistaken, Crabbe and Associates owned a building directly across from Salvatores. No doubt Penelope had an office somewhere near the top floor. A corner window, like his own, he suspected. He scanned the bland bank of windows with an intent gaze.

He'd make a point of asking his investigator to find out which one. Because the next time he confronted Ms. Wentworth, he intended to know every detail about her right down to the shade of lipstick coating that all-too kissable mouth. He wasn't sure how he'd do it, but Penelope wasn't going to marry Robert Cornell any more than she was going to ruin Salvatores by handing over Janus Corp to their chief competitor. Stefano intended to see to it.

Personally.

The first call came through as Penelope glided down the elevator shaft on her way out of Salvatores. It just happened to coincide with the moment she turned her cellular phone back on. The calls continued in an endless stream as she crossed the street to her own office. If she'd had to use her car, she'd have turned the cell phone off again. Ever since a nasty fender-bender that had necessitated a two-day hospital stay, she'd been careful never to combine the two.

It didn't take long to reach her office. "Put everything on hold for the next ten minutes," Penelope instructed her personal assistant as she exited the elevator.

"But, Ms. Wentworth—"

"Please, Cindy. I need ten minutes of peace and quiet and then I'll deal with whatever latest emergency has cropped up since we last spoke."

She didn't wait for a response, but entered her office and firmly closed the door. Leaning against the solid wood panel, she focused on business, hoping to clear the images of Stefano from her mind. It didn't work. This was one aspect of her plan she hadn't taken into consideration.

She'd anticipated a nice, tidy arrangement between the two of them. But her reaction to her intended bridegroom felt anything but tidy. Uncomfortable emotions consumed her from the instant she'd set foot in Stefano's office. And they'd continued long past the moment she'd slid her fingers across his palm and experienced the power and warmth of his handshake. When she'd left his office, she hadn't dared looked back, afraid that she'd lose every ounce of common sense her uncle had instilled over the past sixteen years.

She closed her eyes in frustration. How had Stefano managed to distract her from business?

Maybe his appearance was a factor. She hadn't expected him to be quite so good-looking, despite the photograph her investigator provided. Nor had the report prepared her for the sheer force of his personality. Or perhaps it had been a combination of factors. Perhaps Stefano's powerful disposition combined with the intriguing facts she'd read about him were sufficient to explain her response. Put all his various parts on display in the personal setting of his office and those parts formed a devastating whole.

Damn.

Penelope straightened away from her door. An irritating hint of disinfectant lingered in the room from the janitorial staff's last visit and she wrinkled her nose. Now why did they clean in here every night? It wasn't as though she got it dirty in the short twenty-four hours since their last scrub-fest. Stefano's office hadn't smelled of chemicals. Thinking about it, she couldn't recall any odors other than the delicious scent of his cologne. Why didn't her office smell that nice? She'd have to speak to Cindy about it.

The windows drew her and Penelope crossed the room and swept aside the gauzy curtain that blocked her view of the city. Her gaze focused on Salvatores and she analyzed the building, attempting to determine which window belonged to Stefano. As she recalled it occupied a corner location, similar to her own. He'd had a nice office, totally unlike hers.

A frown lined her brow at the realization. It *was* totally unlike hers. She glanced over her shoulder, her frown deepening. When had all the warmth and character been leeched from the room? Or had it ever been there to start with? And why didn't she have a wall and table covered in personal photos, like Stefano? Or furniture that offered warm, vibrant colors while looking comfortable enough to sleep on?

For some reason, she'd always chosen sedate colors and perfunctory furnishings. For some reason? Her mouth tilted in a wry smile as she acknowledged the truth. She'd chosen her decor based on practicality and sound business sense, just as she based all her decisions. In the past, that had always seemed perfectly logical. But now...

A tentative knock sounded on the door. "Ms. Wentworth?" Cindy hovered at the threshold. "The board's waiting for you."

Penelope gazed out the window for another short moment. *There.* That window. Stefano's office had to be the corner window closest to hers. How ironic, she thought with a silent sigh. And such a shame. A strange longing washed over her. She'd have enjoyed being married to him, even if it would have been a business relationship.

"Ms. Wentworth?"

"Thank you, Cindy," she murmured absently. "Let me get my notes."

"I have them here." Relief edged the PA's voice. "I also have your schedule for the day and the most urgent of your e-mail and phone messages with tentative replies. As soon as you've approved them—"

Penelope paused as she exited her office. "Why don't I ever answer them myself?"

Cindy stared in bewilderment. "You don't have time, Ms. Wentworth."

"You're right." Penelope resumed the short walk toward the conference room. "I don't have time." Nor did she have time for mooning over a gorgeous businessman whose words were flavored with a sexy Italian accent and who had the unmitigated gall to call her *Nellie.* No one had ever called her that. Not ever.

Nor had anyone said her name with such warmth or such a fluid inflection.

"You also won't have a chance to return home this evening before the charity benefit, so I've arranged to have your dress and accessories delivered," Cindy chattered on.

Penelope nodded absentmindedly. Responsibility. Duty. Work ethics. They'd been drummed into her since she'd been a bewildered ten-year-old struggling to come to terms with the death of her parents. "Thank you, Cindy. I appreciate your staying on top of everything."

The PA smiled brightly. "That's what you pay me for—to take care of all of life's nasty details so you can stay focused on business."

Penelope centered her gaze on the hallway leading to the boardroom and kept moving forward. *So she could stay focused on business.* And that said it all, didn't it?

"Hello, Nellie. Small world, isn't it?"

Penelope swung around to face Stefano and he smiled at having caught her by surprise. He liked nudging her off balance. It broke through her rigid control and helped even the score for his ungoverned reaction to her proposition in his office this morning—to her *outrageous* proposition. She stared at him from behind her wire-rimmed glasses, her eyes wide and glittering and far too attractive for his own peace of mind.

He'd noticed her eyes when she'd been in his office, but hadn't realized how utterly bewitching they were. Golden-brown, they gleamed as clear and rich as sunstruck honey, the intense color set off by a ring of unrelenting darkness. She shot him a look as direct as it was apprehensive. Interesting. Why the apprehension? He'd make a point of finding out.

She recovered swiftly. "Mr. Salvatore. This is a surprise."

"Stefano, remember? Actually the surprise is that we've never met before. I'm acquainted with most of the people in this room. I assume you are, too?"

"Yes."

He gestured toward a bubbly blonde on the far side of the room. "Babe Fontaine and her brand-new husband, for instance?"

Penelope inclined her head. She'd worn her hair down for the charity benefit and the loose curls skimmed her bare shoulders in waves of blond and brown and every shade in between. It was an interesting color, he decided. As interesting as the rest of her. The light shimmered within the palest streaks, accentuating the threads of gold.

"I know Reggie quite well," Penelope explained. "I've fronted a few of his business enterprises. I also know Babe's daughter, Sami. She recently married, too."

"I was out of the country so I couldn't attend the ceremony."

"You'd like her husband, Noah. Now that I think about it, you remind me of him."

That snagged his interest. "Remind you...how?"

"You're both tough," she answered instantly. "Hard. Determined. Strong."

Stefano grinned. "You decided all that after one meeting?"

"Yes."

His amusement faded. "Once upon a time people considered me charming. Easygoing. Amusing, even."

She gazed at him once again. *Bewitching.* The word echoed through his mind, a warning as much as it was an observation. "I can see you playing that sort of role. But it isn't the true man."

"And how would you know that?"

Her mouth compressed and she looked away. "Never mind."

Time for a little insight of his own. "Woman's instinct?" When she refused to respond, he leaned forward. A subtle drift of perfume stirred in the air currents between them and his reaction to the feminine scent hit with startling intensity. He didn't remember her wearing it during their business meeting. Just as well, considering the effect it was having. "Or isn't the consummate businesswoman allowed to possess instincts? Perhaps it conflicts with your analytical skills and ability to formulate logical deductions."

He'd guessed right. A hint of chagrin slipped across her expression and her bronze dress rustled in a grumbling whisper. "It's been my experience that facts and figures sway men, not a woman's instincts."

"Is that what your uncle told you?"

She shrugged and the light slid across her shoulders, drawing his attention to the taut, creamy skin bared by her halter neckline. "It's a lesson I learned the hard way. Logic always wins the day." She turned to face him. "Why are you here, Mr. Salvatore?"

She was a lovely woman, her fine-boned appearance deceptive. Just as she'd sensed a hardness in him, he sensed a core of strength that drove her. It would be a mistake to underestimate her ability or determination. "I'm here for the same reason as you."

To his surprise, alarm flared briefly in her gaze before subsiding. "You mean the charity benefit."

"What other reason could there be?"

"None," she lied with blatant disregard.

And that's when he knew. She'd come for another reason. He deliberately switched his attention to the radiant gathering that ebbed and flowed around them. Cornell was here. Somewhere. He'd bet every share of his Salvatore stock. No doubt the delectable Ms. Penelope Wentworth hoped to set up an appointment with him. Fury swept through Stefano, as intense as it was inappropriate. She wasn't betraying him, he fought to remind himself. She wasn't Kate. Penelope had warned him that she'd planned to go to his competitor. Besides, it wasn't as if he wanted to marry her. He simply wanted Janus Corporation.

"You told me I had twenty-four hours, *cara mia*."

"Did you know you speak with an accent whenever you're upset?"

"I hadn't noticed."

"Were you born in Italy?" she persisted.

"No, I was born here. But Italian was our first language. We still speak among ourselves in Italian, fight in Italian, express our emotions in Italian." He lowered his voice to a soft caress. "Make love in Italian."

"Quite reasonable," she retorted with amazing composure. If it hadn't been for the molten flicker of her eyes he might have thought her unaffected.

He stepped closer, not bothering to control the accent that betrayed him. "Most competitors use it as a warning. Perhaps you should, too. Once again, Ms. Wentworth, you told me I had twenty-four hours."

She didn't pretend to misunderstand. "You do."

"You plan to see him tonight, don't you?"

"I was hoping to set up an appointment."

She had every right to make whatever arrangements she chose. He'd turned down her proposal. He had no intention of marrying her. So why the possessive attitude? He couldn't explain it. All he knew was that an irrational annoyance gripped him. It was the thought of

Cornell getting his hands on Janus Corporation, Stefano tried to tell himself. But if that were true, why did an image of Penelope in Cornell's arms taunt him? Just the mere thought of Cornell stripping the thin slip of bronze from her body, of laying her tousled curls on his pillow and covering her body with his was enough to ignite the infamous Salvatore temper.

"You don't know Cornell or you wouldn't go anywhere near the man."

She shrugged. "I've had him investigated, just as I had you investigated, Stefano." She slanted him a teasing glance. "If you want the truth, you were considered the bigger threat."

"Then you hired a fool for an investigator. Either that or Cornell got wind of your activities and rearranged the facts to suit his purpose. He's not a man to fool around with."

"And you are?"

He wished he could explain, could put all the pieces he'd gathered about Cornell into a whole that would give her a true understanding of the man she planned to proposition. But it would take hours. And it would rely on her trusting his gut instincts, something he suspected she'd be loathe to do. Hell, if she didn't trust her own intuition, why would she trust his?

"No," Stefano conceded. "I'm not a man to fool around with. But I wouldn't hurt you. I can't say the same about Cornell."

A hint of amusement drifted into her honey-gold eyes. "Perhaps I gave you the wrong impression about this marriage. I wasn't planning on giving myself heart and soul to the man I marry." She regarded him with calm deliberation. "It's temporary. No consummation, no strings or marital obligations, remember?"

He dropped his hands onto her shoulders. The supple muscles of her arms tensed beneath his palm, her skin as soft and fluid as the finest silk. He urged her closer until she locked against him in a perfect fit. Then he lowered his head, his mouth a scant inch away from her ear.

"Listen to me, Nellie, and listen well. With Cornell, you won't have any choice. He takes what he wants and discards it when he grows bored. He'll make you a part of the agreement no matter what he promises."

Her breath stirred the air between them. "Me? What do you mean?"

"Use your imagination."

Apparently she possessed an active one, despite a logical turn of mind. Distaste followed on the heels of comprehension. "You don't know that for certain," she protested.

"Yes, I do. If you tell him you don't want to consummate the marriage, you'll rouse his hunter's instinct. He'll take you down because it's a challenge he won't be able to resist. And if you say nothing, he'll make you his if only to put his stamp on you. And when he's satisfied that there's nothing more he considers novel or interesting, he'll get rid of you on his terms and in as public and humiliating a way as possible."

She jerked free of his hold and he didn't attempt to restrain her further. "You're lying. You're saying that so I won't approach him."

"You're right. I am telling you this so you won't approach him. But it's not a lie."

"How do you know?"

"That's not open for discussion. You can trust me or not. Your choice. But I'm warning you. Go to Cornell and you'll regret it."

"Don't you understand?" she protested. "I have no choice."

"Sure you do." How could such a smart woman be so dense? "You have the option of finding a man you can love. Of pursuing a real marriage. Do things the old-fashioned way."

"It wouldn't work. All the men I know expect to marry Penelope Wentworth."

He lifted an eyebrow at that. "And they wouldn't be?"

She faced him with a defiance that transfigured her. Gone was the cool, rational businesswoman who'd invaded his office. In her place stood a beacon of flame, fierce and emotional and more desirable than he'd have thought possible. "They want the corporation. Not the individual. They want high finance and business dinners and dealing with the movers and shakers."

"They want Penelope, instead of Nellie. Is that it?"

She stared at him with something akin to shock. "Yes," she whispered. "That's exactly what I mean."

Stefano didn't say a word. To admit he wanted Nellie more than Penelope would give her false hopes. He had no intention of marrying her or anyone else. "Don't do it, *cara*. Don't go to Cornell."

He thought he'd gotten through to her. But at the last instant, she shook her head. "I need to marry. And I need to do it sooner rather than later."

With that, she turned and disappeared into the crowd. Stefano let her go. After all...

She wasn't his to stop.

Penelope walked briskly across the ballroom, as though she had a specific destination in mind. Not that she did, other than to put as much distance between herself and

Stefano. She'd definitely take him off her list of prospective bridegrooms. He was all wrong. Too controlling. Too demanding. Too insightful. She shivered. Too passionately Italian. It would be illogical to choose him over a more amenable sort of man.

If only she didn't find him so darned attractive.

"Penelope?" She turned to discover her uncle beside her. He acknowledged her distracted expression with a curious look. "I've been looking for you."

"Sorry, Uncle Loren." She linked arms with him. "I had people to see."

"You never let a business opportunity slip by, do you?" he asked fondly.

She gave his arm a gentle squeeze. "I learned from the best."

"Who was that man I saw you talking to? A potential client?"

"His name's Stefano Salvatore. We met recently." Since prevarication wasn't part of her nature and never would be, she added, "To be honest, he's not a client."

"He's a...friend? You were having a rather heated discussion with him. Was there a problem?"

"We were talking about Janus Corporation."

Loren nodded, relaxing ever so slightly. "Ah, yes. That's where I recall the name. The Salvatores have been interested in acquiring that particular business for some time now. I also have a vague memory of a scandal involving one of them. Or do I have that wrong?"

"Unfounded rumors." She dismissed the accusation as though it were of no consequence. "It's all an unfortunate misunderstanding. I believe I'll step in and sort it out, if you don't mind."

"It's none of our affair."

"No doubt. However, I believe I'll make it our affair."

An unmistakable determination underscored her comment and Loren released his breath in a gusty sigh. "I'm too familiar with that tone to argue. You always did have a regrettable weak spot for underdogs."

"Stefano is far from an underdog. He'll resolve this problem on his own at some point. I'm just hoping to speed up the process." She slanted her uncle a thoughtful gaze. "What do you know about the Salvatores? Do they run an ethical business?"

"I don't recall any rumors of unethical behavior—other than this one incident. If I remember correctly, the Salvatores have always maintained an excellent reputation. Why?"

She gave a brisk nod. "That's my impression, too. I just wanted your take on the firm since I trust your judgment in these matters. And what about Robert Cornell? Have you ever met him?"

Her uncle hesitated. "Yes."

"And?"

"A very astute businessman."

"What about on a more personal level?"

Her uncle's brows pulled together. "Why the sudden interest in Salvatore and Cornell? Is this business related or personal?"

"Both. Humor me, Uncle Loren. Consider the two on a purely impartial basis. If you had to trust one or the other, whom would you choose?"

"And my choices are Salvatore and..."

"Cornell."

"Stick with Salvatore."

"I was afraid you'd say that," she murmured.

She glanced toward Stefano. He was talking to a stun-

ning redhead, smiling in a way that filled Penelope with
a peculiar longing. She trusted her uncle's instincts as
much as her own ability to sift and weigh and analyze.
Although on the surface, Cornell seemed the more trust-
worthy of the two, certain elements didn't add up.
Perhaps it was because all the information she had on
him appeared too perfect. She'd never trusted total perfection. It rarely lived up to its press. That combined
with Stefano's warning…

It didn't take long to evaluate her options. She'd give
Mr. Salvatore one last try, she decided. If he turned her
proposition down flat, she'd search out Cornell and
judge the man for herself. Perhaps perfect on paper really did mean perfect. And even if the man was flawed,
she could work with flawed. She grinned. After all, she'd
planned to work with Stefano and he was most decid-
edly, arrogantly, deliciously flawed.

Marching across the floor, she reached Stefano's side
and slipped a hand beneath his arm. It took every ounce
of nerve to smile at the redhead as though she didn't
have a care in the world while tucking herself tight
against the man she'd claimed. He glanced down at her
with a puzzled expression.

"I thought we could discuss my proposition a little
further," she murmured in a sultry voice that would have
shocked her fellow board members if they'd heard.

But, darn it all! Sometimes logic just didn't belong.
And she suspected this was one of those few times.
Unfortunately the voice was all she had. No doubt a
seduction lesson or two would have been far more help-
ful at this particular juncture than so many finance
classes. Ironic, considering she'd never felt the need to
seduce a man before.

"Something you forgot to tell me, darling?" the red-head asked Stefano.

"*Amorata.*" He held out the hand Penelope had left unfettered. "*Bellissima. Moglie mia.* I swear. I've never even seen this woman before in my life."

Penelope's mouth dropped open. "Never... I don't believe this! Are you going to stand here and tell me—tell *her*—we've never met?"

"Yes." His head bobbed up and down. "Never."

"Oh, and I suppose I wasn't in your office earlier today propositioning you?"

Stefano muttered something in Italian, before carefully disengaging his arm and hastening to the redhead's side. "She must be insane. Please, Hanna, don't hold it against her."

To her amazement, Hanna simply smiled, her amusement indicating a woman secure in her position. She tucked her hand through Stefano's arm in a manner identical to the one Penelope had used. "I think I know what's going on."

Well, Penelope sure as heck didn't. She planted her hands on her hips and scowled at the two. "Stefano Salvatore. I proposed marriage to you less than twelve hours ago. Are you going to stand there and deny it?"

The two stared at her, torn between laughter and shock. "Marriage?"

"That's it." Penelope retreated behind her most businesslike facade—the one she reserved for the grittiest board meetings. "You can forget the twenty-four-hour grace period, Mr. Salvatore. It's been rescinded. As far as I'm concerned, our business ends now. I'm going to find Cornell."

She spun around and slammed into an impressive wall

of chest. Her gaze shifted upward, clashing with a pair of smoldering dark brown eyes—a very familiar pair of smoldering dark brown eyes.

"Uh-oh," she murmured.

CHAPTER THREE

STEFANO dropped a heavy hand on her shoulder, steadying her. "Hello, *cara*."

"Stefano?" Penelope whispered.

"In the flesh."

She glanced behind her and winced. "If you're Stefano, then who…?"

"Allow me to introduce you to my twin brother, Marco, and his wife, Hanna."

"No, thank you," she managed with remarkable composure. "I believe I'll just go slink into the most convenient corner and suffer my humiliation in private."

"I don't think so." Grasping her shoulders, he spun her around to suffer her humiliation in all too public a fashion. "Marco, Hanna, I'd like to introduce you to Penelope Wentworth. She owns Crabbe and Associates."

"I gather Penelope is your new fiancée?" Hanna asked irrepressibly. "Your father will be thrilled."

"She's *not* my fiancée, new or otherwise."

"Gee, that isn't what she told us."

"Enough, *amorata*," Marco interrupted. "We should leave them to discuss their differences in private." He shot his brother a broad grin. "We can grill him later. Maybe he can give us a few of the more interesting details during the next Salvatores' board meeting. That way he won't have to repeat the story a half-dozen times."

Stefano's fingers bit into her shoulders and Penelope

winced. To her astonishment he directed a harsh flood of Italian toward his brother. Judging by Hanna's expression, it was probably a good thing Penelope didn't understand a word of it. The instant he finished, he swept her across the room. People moved out of their way, suspicion and dislike in the gazes that settled on Stefano, surprise in the gazes that landed on her.

Heaven help him! Penelope thought, horrified. Was this the sort of treatment he received on a regular basis? She had a terrible feeling it was. She slanted him a quick, concerned glance. How could he stand coming to these functions? It must be sheer torture.

They walked through the nearest doorway, which led onto a balcony overlooking the San Francisco Bay. Lights glittered along the sweep of the Golden Gate and Bay Bridges and dotted the darkness of the water. If it weren't for the fury emanating from the man beside her she'd have found the view as relaxing as it was picturesque. A faint glow illuminated Stefano's features, gilding the angles with moonlight. It gave a harsh beauty to his appearance, a stern remoteness she'd never seen before. She tugged against his hold.

"You can let go of me now."

He did as she requested, allowing for a meager inch or two of breathing space. She'd hoped his releasing her would have stopped the awareness slamming through her. It didn't, and the unexpected sensation confused her. She'd worked with men all her life and had never experienced such an overwhelming attraction. Why did it have to happen with Stefano? She suppressed a groan. What a pickle! This would make for a most inconvenient marriage.

"What the *hell* did you think you were doing?" he finally demanded.

Penelope wrapped her arms around her waist. "I was giving you a final chance before approaching Cornell."

"By propositioning my *brother?* What is it? Any Salvatore is acceptable, even the married ones?"

"Oh, cut it out, Stefano." She shot him her most quelling look. It didn't do the least bit of good. He continued to regard her with one of his more intimidating glares. Not that she was intimidated. Not a chance. "Why do men always leap to the most absurd conclusions when confronting women?"

"For your information, *cara,* being upset because you propositioned my brother, isn't the least absurd. It's downright reasonable."

"Reasonable?" She experienced an irrational flash of anger. When was the last time she'd lost her temper? She couldn't even remember. Planting her hands on her hips, she glared at Stefano. "It is not the least reasonable to be upset. For your information, *I did not proposition Marco.*" She cleared her throat. "Not exactly."

"What 'exactly' would you call it?"

"You're being deliberately obtuse. You know I thought Marco was you. It was…" She lifted her chin. "It was a natural error. Perfectly understandable."

"Meaning you couldn't tell the two of us apart. What happened to your impressive ability to weigh, analyze and deduce?"

Her hands collapsed into fists, anger shattering her composure. How did he do it? How did he manage, with a few choice words, to decimate years of experience controlling her emotions? "In case no one's bothered to mention it, you two are identical twins. Deduce that, if you would."

"Hanna could tell the difference between us."

"Oh, that's totally unfair! Hanna's married to Marco.

I'd hope she could tell the difference between the two of you."

"She could tell from the beginning," Stefano maintained stubbornly. "The first time we met she knew I wasn't Marco."

"Well, bully for her!" Penelope paced in front of him, her glasses bouncing on the tip of her nose with each infuriated step. Muttering impatiently, she shoved them into her hair and out of the way. Her poor vision caused Stefano to appear blurred around the edges when she looked in his direction. But for now, she preferred him a bit blurry. "I've met you precisely once and that's supposed to be enough to distinguish you from your brother?"

"You saw the photos in my office of the two of us. You knew I had a twin. You're a smart woman, a virtual female Sherlock Holmes with your logic this and analyze that. You couldn't have utilized a portion of your infamous deductive skills in order to uncover your mistake?"

"I did uncover my mistake!"

"Sure you did. The instant you body-slammed me. A little late in the day, considering you'd already let slip about that ridiculous marriage proposal."

She understood then. "That's why you're so mad, isn't it? You're upset that they know I proposed to you."

"Yes."

Now that she'd figured out what had set him off, her temper cooled a trifle. It came as an immense relief. She didn't like losing control. "Just tell them it was a business proposition and that you refused me," she suggested. "That's simple enough, isn't it?"

"You don't know my family, or you wouldn't say that. Do I need to remind you that I have five brothers?"

She stared blankly.

"Hello? *Five* brothers. Five brothers who won't let this go without having something to say about it."

"Oh, I get it." She dismissed his concern with a careless shrug. "So they'll tease you a little. I assume that's what brothers do? I never had any so I admit, I'm unfamiliar with the process."

He eyed her in a way that suggested they'd be talking about her background in greater detail at some point in the future. "I'm used to being teased," he informed her. "That doesn't bother me. What does have me concerned is what will happen when word leaks as to *why* you propositioned me. What happens when your uncle gets wind of your activities?"

"Is that likely? Your family will—"

"Take great delight in discussing it. Discussing it at length, I might add. That's often accompanied by the occasional eavesdropping secretary or visitor. My family won't deliberately leak the information, but these things have a way of getting out."

She frowned. "Uncle Loren will be hurt if he hears about my marital plans from an outside source."

"I suspect he'll be more than hurt. I suspect he'll be flat-out furious. I also suspect he'll do everything he can to stop you."

It was a distinct possibility. Loren had controlled the reins of her corporation for a lot of years. He was accustomed to it, enjoyed it, planned to continue for a long time to come. And she would have been perfectly happy to let him if...

"You don't understand, Stefano. Once I'm married—"

He cut her off again. "Once you're married, you'll have control of an infuriated board. I doubt they'll understand or sympathize with your need to take over. How will a power struggle affect your business? Or don't you care?''

"Of course I care. It's my company we're talking about.''

"Then I suggest you leave everything status quo. You've said your uncle's doing a good job. Let him continue doing a good job.''

"You don't understand.''

"No, I don't.'' He crossed to stand beside her, resting his arms along the railing of the balcony. His anger faded, but the tension remained, implicit in the taut set of his shoulders and rigid length of his spine. "Look, Nellie. I can't pretend to understand the relationship you have with your uncle, but in my family, Salvatores stick together. Loyalty is everything to us. We don't go behind each others' backs and we don't act in a way contrary to what's in our collective best interests.''

"There are facts not in your possession.''

He glanced over his shoulder at her, his mouth twitching into a smile at her phrasing. "I assume these facts would influence my opinion?''

"Yes.''

"I'll also assume you don't intend to give me all the facts?''

"No more than you intend to give me all your facts regarding Robert Cornell.''

He remained silent for a moment before asking, "I take it you're still planning to proposition him?''

"I don't have a choice.''

"Mind if I make a suggestion?'' He didn't wait for her answer. "Don't tell him the purpose of your meeting. At least, not the true purpose. Don't propose to him in that initial get-together like you did to me.''

"Why not?"

He turned to stare out to sea again, his remoteness belied by the iron-tight grip he maintained on the railing. "Get a sense of the man first. Will you do that much?"

"What if my uncle hears about my meeting with him? How will I explain it?"

"What if your uncle hears about *our* meeting? I suspect you'll have even more trouble explaining that, especially considering my reputation."

"Your reputation doesn't worry me."

"It should," he bit out.

She approached, joining him at the railing. "As I've told you, I don't believe you're guilty. Therefore your reputation has no bearing on my actions or decisions. What I need to know is…can you keep Marco and Hanna from talking?"

"For a short while."

"A short while is all that's necessary." It was time to wrap up their meeting. If she stayed with him any longer, she'd be tempted to do something incredibly stupid. Like beg him to marry her. "I owe you an apology, Stefano. I've made matters awkward for you with your family."

"I'll survive."

"I also appreciate your suggestions."

"No charge."

She smiled at that. "Well…" She offered her hand. "Thanks again."

His fingers swallowed hers. "Just so you know, Nellie… There's something about all this that doesn't add up. I know it. You know it. And Cornell won't be fooled, either."

She stared, momentarily stunned. Oh, dear. How in the world had she given herself away? She released a silent sigh. Not that the entire situation wasn't suspicious enough in and of itself. "I have no idea what you're talking about," she managed to say with a modicum of serenity.

"Sure you do. You're just unwilling to explain." His mouth slanted upward in a dangerous smile. "But I'll figure it out."

"You won't have the opportunity, remember? I'll be seeing Robert Cornell tomorrow."

He didn't bother arguing further. "So you've said."

"And…and you're finished with the whole business, right? You've made your decision, so I'm free to approach someone else?"

"It's a free country, *cara*." His gaze intensified. "Or were you asking my permission?"

"Of course not." She glanced toward the light streaming from the ballroom. "I should go now."

She took a single step in the direction of the doorway before he stopped her. Catching her around the waist, he swung her into his arms. "When you go to Cornell, you should take one final point into consideration."

She read the determination in his gaze and knew what he intended. "You're going to kiss me, aren't you?"

"The thought crossed my mind."

Her response was instantaneous. Never had she felt so aware, so alive, her senses sharper than she could ever remember experiencing. Not even in the most spirited board meetings had she been this sensitive to every nuance in a man's voice, every inflection in every word, every look and breath and expression.

"And what's the kiss supposed to prove? Am I supposed to find you more attractive than Cornell? Should I let him kiss me, too, so I can compare?"

Stefano's eyes caught fire. "I'd rather you didn't."

"Why? You don't want me."

"I didn't say that." He cradled her close, holding her as though she were infinitely precious. "I said I didn't want to marry you in order to acquire Janus Corporation."

She relished the forbidden sensation. Her entire life had been spent in the pursuit of the appropriate and necessary. This was neither of those things. And in that moment she found she craved it more than anything else in the world. "Okay, Stefano. Go ahead and kiss me. But it won't prove a thing."

"No?" His breath grazed her temple, catching in the soft waves of her hair. It was the most subtle of caresses. A touch without touching. She shivered in anticipation. "I think it'll prove something very important."

As he spoke, he splayed her arms outward, away from her sides. A wash of cool air funneled in, stealing away the warmth of his touch. She wished she could close the distance between them, but his silent request was implicit. He wanted her to hold the position. Unable to resist, she stood acquiescent, waiting to see what he intended. He didn't keep her waiting for long.

Murmuring what could only have been an Italian endearment, he leaned in. He still didn't take her in his arms, though his warmth returned, eclipsing the cool sea air and splashing across her skin in delicious waves of scented heat. Just when she thought she couldn't bare it a moment longer, he reached for her. It was a butterfly touch, the very tips of his fingers skimming with featherlight strokes. He traced a leisurely path across her bared shoulder blades and down her arms to the center of her palms, arousing her with stunning ease.

She shuddered in reaction, and a delicious lassitude radiated to the very depths of her being. How was that possible? How could he kindle such intense passion with only the most subtle physical contact? She moistened her lips, swaying closer, desperate to know his full embrace. Darn it all! Why didn't he yank her into his arms and kiss the hell out of her?

"You still haven't explained," she said, fighting for coherency. "What will kissing me prove?"

His hands trailed a path of fire back upward, branding her all over again. "Nellie. *Cara mia.*" His thumbs brushed her cheekbones. "Look at me."

She didn't want to look. That would force her to think about what he was doing, force her to take action instead of allowing him to determine the full depth and scope of their embrace. "Please, Stefano." *Kiss me, dammit!*

"What are you feeling, Nellie? What are you thinking?"

She opened one eye. "To be honest, I'm feeling pretty darned desperate. And I'm thinking that if you don't do something about it soon, I might have to show you how it's done."

She shut her eyes again and waited as an impossibly long minute ticked by. *When was he going to kiss her?* Unable to contain her impatience, she peeked up at him. Passion marked his face, the male aggression as blatant as she'd ever seen it. But he made no move to act on his desire.

"You want my kiss, don't you?" The quiet urgency in his voice only served to underscore the strength of his need.

"Yes, I want it," honesty compelled her to admit. "Very much, if you don't mind. And soon. Like now."

He didn't take the hint. "That should tell you that it's more than a business alliance you're after. In fact, I'm willing to bet that business is the last thing on your mind.''

"You'd win that bet," she muttered.

"Don't you understand? You want something else. You *need* something more. Don't settle for less than a full relationship."

Curiosity consumed her. "Did you? With your ex-fiancée, I mean? Is that the point of this demonstration?"

"Dammit, woman." She'd asked the wrong question. Darkness descended in his gaze and the mouth she'd hoped to explore as thoroughly as humanly possible compressed into a straight line. "You really are determined to annoy me, aren't you?"

"It's not deliberate." Her chuckle rumbled in the air between them. "I believe Uncle Loren describes it as a talent."

"Have you listened to a word I've said?"

"I've listened to all of them. Right up until you said you were going to kiss me. Then I was hoping you'd replace words with action." She grinned. "You can take that as a serious request, by the way."

"So I gathered."

Ever so gently he slid her glasses from her hair and placed them on the tip of her nose. Penelope sighed in disappointment. "You're not going to kiss me, are you?"

"Smart woman."

A small noise coming from the direction of the ballroom distracted her and she glanced over Marco's shoulder. Bill Marks, the organizer of the charity benefit stood in the doorway of the balcony, watching them. "Hello, Bill," she called. "Looking for someone?"

He hesitated for a second, then nodded. "As a matter of fact, I was. I'd like to speak to Mr. Salvatore."

"Listen to me, Nellie," Stefano said in an undertone. "I need you to leave. Now."

She glanced from one man to the other. "Why?"

"I don't want you caught in the middle of this."

"In the middle of—" Comprehension hit and she spun around to regard Marks with a suspicious, narrow-eyed stare. "What's going on, Bill?"

"Ms. Wentworth, please. I'd prefer to speak to Mr. Salvatore in private."

"I don't doubt that for a minute." She took up a defiant stance in front of Stefano and folded her arms across her chest. "But I'm not leaving. So I suggest you tell me what's going on."

Stefano dropped his hands to her shoulders. "Don't interfere. This is my problem and I'll deal with it."

"But—"

"He's come to ask me to leave, as I'm sure you're aware." He gently propelled her out of the way. "I don't hide behind women, Penelope. Nor do I allow them to stand in the line of fire when someone comes gunning for me."

Penelope. He'd called her Penelope. That hurt more than anything else he could have said. It also infuriated her. "Is Mr. Salvatore right?" Beside her Stefano muttered a short word in Italian. It did not sound complimentary. "Are you here to ask him to leave, Bill?"

The poor man looked most unhappy. "I'm afraid so. As the organizer of the event, I'm required to take care of the situation. If it were up to me…" He shrugged. "But it isn't. And since this is for charity, we can't afford even the appearance of—"

Penelope smiled sweetly. "Impropriety?"

"Yes."

A sudden thought occurred. "Is it all the Salvatores or just this Salvatore?"

The split-second hesitation gave Marks away. Stefano stiffened beside her and she could practically smell the fierce aggression take hold at the threat to his family. "Who's behind this?" Whereas before his lilting Italian accent had stroked each word, now it hardened into fierce demand, a whip instead of a caress.

"No one. Everyone! I really can't say, Mr. Salvatore. I've simply been asked to deal with the situation."

"Who asked you? Give me a name."

"I can't do that. I'm sorry. It would mean my job."

Penelope decided to step in again. No doubt it would rile Stefano, but that couldn't be helped. "I'm disappointed in you, Mr. Marks. Crabbe and Associates, as well as Salvatores, has always been happy to support these benefits. I see we'll have to reassess our position."

"Please, Ms. Wentworth. I'd rather you didn't do that. You've always been quite generous."

"Tell me...has there ever been the appearance of impropriety as far as my company is concerned?"

"Never!"

"And if I vouch for the Salvatores?"

"I told you not to interfere, *cara*," Stefano interrupted.

She kept her gaze trained on Marks as she replied. "This might be a good time for you to learn I don't take instruction well. I'm much more accustomed to giving it." A sudden idea occurred—the perfect solution to their problem. "I know. We'll dance."

"Excuse me?"

"We'll dance." She faced him, offering a broad, satisfied smile. "You and I. After that, I'll dance with all of your brothers while Uncle Loren dances with their wives. And we'll laugh. A lot. We'll also talk to a few key individuals who have enough influence to put an end to any further comments for the evening, and will be only too willing to cooperate if they wish to continue doing business with my firm."

"Don't put yourself in the middle," Stefano warned. "You might find you don't have as much influence as you'd hoped."

Her smile faded. "Do you remember when you asked me to trust your judgment on a certain matter of mutual interest?" She asked the question with pointed delicacy.

He sighed. "You want me to trust yours now?"

"I'll make a deal with you. I'll do as you suggested. I won't approach this particular business deal the same way I did today."

"And in exchange?"

Her smile returned, even more brilliant than before. "We dance." She glanced at Marks. "Bill, I suggest you wait here for a little while. Enjoy the view. I don't think you'll need to worry about the appearance of impropriety any further this evening."

"Thank you, Ms. Wentworth. I suspect you're right."

"Yes, I suspect I'm right, too. I usually am. And you're quite welcome." She slipped a hand into the crook of Stefano's elbow and walked with him toward the ballroom. "Now then, Mr. Salvatore… Where were we before we were so rudely interrupted?"

"I was leaving and you were going to set up your appointment with Cornell," Stefano answered promptly.

She slanted him a speaking look. "That's not my recollection. I seem to remember you were going to kiss me."

"As I recall I was going to *not* kiss you. For once in my life I'd planned to play it safe."

"A pity."

His mouth curved into a wry smile. "My feelings, precisely."

"Do you suppose dancing would be playing it safe?"

"With you? I sincerely doubt it."

She doubted it, as well. Still... It wouldn't be anywhere near as exciting as kissing Stefano Salvatore. Darn it all. She suspected it would have been an enjoyable activity before getting married and bringing an end to any further pleasure.

Stefano glanced at the woman clinging to his arm. He'd wanted to kiss her. He'd held her in his arms and been consumed with the urge to cover her mouth with his and explore the warm, silken depths. She wouldn't have resisted. No, she'd wanted it as much as he had. So what had stopped him?

He knew what. The slight shock had reverberated through her body at his touch combined with the sheer astonishment in her brilliant golden eyes had made him hesitate. For one brief moment, he'd jarred her from her goal, had forced her to acknowledge him as a man instead of a solution to her business problem. The fact should have pleased him.

Instead it had made him wary.

Penelope had an untouched air about her that scared him spitless—a Sleeping Beauty awaiting true love's kiss. And he wasn't about to be the one to awaken her. Not while his reputation stood in ruins. It wouldn't be fair to either of them. In fact, if it hadn't been for this latest threat to the Salvatore business as a whole, he'd never have allowed Penelope to proceed with her current plan. He'd have simply left.

But someone out there intended to destroy his family's business. And he wasn't about to let that happen.

He regarded the crowd through fierce eyes. Whoever it was should have stuck with ruining him. Because the moment they'd attacked his family, they'd made a fatal mistake.

No one messed with what belonged to him.

He glanced down at Penelope. "I promise, *cara*. You won't be harmed by this. If anyone tries—"

"Let me guess." She slipped into his arms with an innate feminine grace and elegance that aroused all that was most elementally male in him. "You'll make him pay. Just as you'll make him pay for what he's trying to do to your family."

He swung her onto the dance floor, his expression easing from ferocious to indulgent. "You know me so well?"

"Nowhere near well enough," Penelope muttered beneath her breath.

And nowhere near as well as she would have if he'd kissed her. She'd wanted that kiss with a desperation alien to her nature. Stefano had held her in his arms and she'd been overwhelmed with the urge to explore every inch of that fascinating mouth. The minute he'd touched her, every thought but one had consumed her. To revel in the intimacy of his kiss. To wallow in the wealth of emotions his touch inspired. So why had he stopped?

She could guess.

He didn't want her. She'd barged into his office and proposed marriage. Or rather, she'd proposed a business arrangement. Was he afraid that if he kissed her he'd be obligated to accept her offer? Or was he simply not interested in her on any level, business or personal?

It didn't matter, she told herself stoically. In fact, it was all for the best. For the briefest of moments she'd lost sight of her goal. That had never happened to her before. Never. Clearly Stefano Salvatore was a dangerous man and it would be a serious mistake to involve him in her scheme to gain control of Crabbe and Associates. She couldn't afford to be distracted. Not if she hoped to succeed.

She sighed, snuggling close to Stefano. It was a shame really. She'd never met anyone who could distract her before. It might have been interesting to find out just how distracted she could have become.

CHAPTER FOUR

STEFANO stared at his brothers in disbelief. "You're kidding."

"No, we're not kidding." Luc, the oldest of the six, took the lead. "The timing couldn't be better. We've been talking about expansion. Dom's in Italy so we don't have to worry about any paternal disapproval. You said yourself she was offering a business arrangement—"

"You want me to marry a woman I don't know or love so we can expand our business interests?"

"No," Luc retorted. "We want you to marry Ms. Wentworth so Cornell doesn't put us out of business. Expanding is a bonus. If she planned to approach anyone else, I'd let it go. But Cornell plays dirty."

"Would it be such a hardship?" Marco interrupted. "She seemed quite interested in you last night."

Stefano glared at his twin. "No. She seemed quite interested in *you.*"

"Details." Marco waved that aside. "The point is…she's attracted. And she'd much rather give us her business than Cornell. Why disappoint her?"

"She plans to take control of her corporation away from her uncle."

Exasperated, Marco tossed his pen onto his legal pad. "So? They're her companies."

Stefano thrust back from the conference table and stood. His brothers had blindsided him and he didn't like it one little bit. He crossed to the bank of windows overlooking the city of San Francisco, his focus inevitably turning to Penelope's building. He scowled. "Her uncle has been running Crabbe and Associates for years. He knows what he's doing."

"Penelope's determined to marry," Luc pointed out with annoying logic. "And from what little you've told us, she'll accomplish her goal whether it's by marrying you or marrying someone else. Why not profit from this?"

"Would you do it?" Stefano demanded over his shoulder.

"I'm already married."

"Come on, Luc. You know what I mean. If you weren't married to Grace, would you marry a stranger for profit?"

"It's a moot point," Marco answered for his brother, "since you're attracted to her. Come on, Stef. Admit it. You want her."

Stefano's mouth tightened. "What has that got to do with anything?"

"You've only met her a while ago and she already has you tied up in knots." Marco grinned. "That's how it was when I first met Hanna. I knew."

"I'm not in love with the woman," he bit out. "It would be like falling in love with...with a *computer*."

Marco shrugged. "Hanna was obsessed with business, too. It's your job to show her there's more to life than work. I have every confidence you can do it, too."

"Consider the alternatives," Luc added. "Stop and think what it would mean to Salvatores if Cornell got his hands on Janus Corp."

"I suppose it's too much to hope that Cornell will turn her down flat?"

Luc shook his head. "He'd find her offer irresistible. He'd marry her just for the novelty of the situation."

Stefano couldn't argue with fact. But Luc's comment disturbed him, reminding him of something she'd said last night. What had it been? Something about the men she knew wanting Penelope, not Nellie. They wanted what she could bring to the marriage, rather than the person. He gritted his teeth. Cornell would be no different. If anything he'd be far worse. The mere thought of her sacrificing herself to a man like that—

"How long do you think it would take him to bring us to our knees?" Luc urged, no doubt sensing weakness.

"Not long," Alessandro announced, walking into the conference room. As the second brother, he was the tallest and broadest of the Salvatores. He was also the most grim, with pitiless eyes and a hardness few cared to confront. "It's worse than we thought."

"How much worse?" Stefano demanded.

"Cornell was behind the incident last night. Not only did he demand that Marks remove Stefano, he also claimed that new evidence has come to light and all of the Salvatores are suspected of having been involved in that incident with the Bennetts."

"We'll sue!"

"To hell with the courts," Pietro protested. "Let's go pay Cornell a visit and explain the error of his ways in person."

Rocco flexed his fists. "I'm ready."

"No," Luc interrupted. "We have a better way of taking care of Cornell. One that will put him out of business permanently. Isn't that right, Stefano?"

Stefano could feel the net tightening around him.

"What happened to the Salvatore claim that we only marry for love?"

"You won't be the first to disprove that," Alessandro interrupted. "I'm one step ahead of you."

"And two divorces in the family will make it any more acceptable? At least you married for love, even if it didn't work."

Marco approached and dropped a heavy hand on Stefano's shoulder. "And you won't?" he demanded in an undertone. "There's something between you and this Wentworth woman. I realize it's too soon to call it love. But what if it is? What if your feelings for her could develop over time. If she marries Cornell you won't have the chance to know for sure."

Stefano shrugged off the comment. "You're dreaming."

"They are pleasant dreams, yes?"

"Marco—"

"If you're still not convinced, consider this... She stood up for us last night. She danced with every single one of us, putting her reputation on the line. That won't sit well with Cornell. When he finds out what she wants from him, he'll marry her. He'll take her company." His expression turned grim. "And then he'll make her pay for daring to interfere."

Marco was right and Stefano knew it. There wasn't a doubt in his mind that Cornell had been in a fury the night before. He hadn't made any attempt to disguise it, which had prompted Alessandro's investigation.

Stefano owed Penelope. Hell, the whole family owed her. She'd done just as she'd promised by dancing with them, even insisting they all stay until the bitter end, laughing and joking and acting as if they didn't have a care in the world. She'd been a particular hit with the three wives, Carina, Grace and Hanna. By the end of the evening they'd been in a tight knot, chattering intimately with one another as though they were all lifelong friends.

And throughout that endless night, Stefano had longed to steal Penelope away from his family and sweep her onto the balcony to finish what they'd started there. To hold her in his arms and kiss her senseless. Kiss her until she'd forgotten all about Cornell and Janus Corp and her insane quest for a husband.

He glared at the office window his investigator had indicated belonged to Penelope. How could he allow her to assume the risk she seemed so determined to take? She might have been participating in the corporate world these past sixteen years, but clearly, she didn't have a clue when it came to someone like Cornell. She was accustomed to a board who obeyed, who didn't dare get down and dirty with the owner of the company paying their salary. But more important than that… How could he let Cornell touch her?

Simple. He couldn't.

"Fine." Stefano swung around to face his family. "I'll approach her again. I'm not promising to marry the woman, but I'll try to secure her promise to sell us Janus."

"You'll speak to her before she meets with Cornell?"

"I'm not a fool." Stefano closed his eyes. *Just an idiot!* "I'll call her."

"Better yet, go and see her," Marco urged. "Use some of that Salvatore charm."

"She doesn't like charm. She told me so."

"Then use logic. And if that doesn't work…"

"What?"

Marco grinned. "Try giving her that kiss she asked for last night."

*   *   *

Stefano hadn't come. Penelope released her breath in a regretful sigh. She'd hoped he would, hoped he'd decide that the advantages of marriage to her outweighed the disadvantages. Some secret part of her had been certain that his desire to get his hands on Janus would be stronger than his distaste for her proposal.

Impulsively she rang through to her PA. "Have there been any messages?"

"Fourteen phone calls and nineteen e-mails."

"Are any from—"

"None are from Mr. Salvatore. I'm sorry, Ms. Wentworth."

The sympathy in Cindy's voice returned the steel to Penelope's backbone. "I'll be leaving for Benjamin's now to meet with Cornell. If my uncle asks for me, please inform him I'm out to lunch with a prospective client. Under no circumstances are you to tell him who I'm with or where I am."

"Yes, Ms. Wentworth. And if Mr. Salvatore phones?"

"He won't."

Returning the receiver to its cradle, Penelope stood and straightened her suit jacket. Gathering up her purse, she gave her office one final look. Maybe she should consider some new furniture. Just a few bits and pieces in warm, earthy tones with splashes of vibrant, jewel tones. And some photographs. A couple of choice family pictures of her parents and Uncle Loren scattered on the wall and coffee table. She made a mental note to mention it to Cindy and then instantly changed her mind. No, this would be one of life's "nasty details" she'd handle herself.

After all, it was about time.

*   *   *

"Where is she?"

"I'm sorry, sir. Ms. Wentworth isn't available."

"She is to me."

Stefano brushed past Penelope's assistant and shoved open the door leading to his soon-to-be fiancée's office. The room was empty. Unable to help himself, he entered, examining the decor with a vague sensation of concern. It felt cold and stark. Functional. Not a single personal memento marred the various surfaces and even the colors left him with an impression of untouched remoteness. The entire room screamed, "business only." As her PA had warned, Penelope had gone, leaving behind a delicious trail of the same subtle perfume she'd worn the night before.

Now that, he decided grimly, wasn't "business only."

"Where is she?" he asked the assistant.

"Sir, I can't—"

He turned to face her. "Let me make this easier for you. I'm Stefano Salvatore. Nellie and I have…an arrangement pending. I'm forced to assume that because I'm late getting back to her, she's gone to meet Cornell for lunch. Am I correct so far?"

The assistant's expression gave him his answer.

"Then all I need from you is when and where."

"I can't give you that information. It'll mean my job."

"We can't have that happen," he acknowledged.

He thought fast. Now where would someone like Nellie take a prospective bridegroom? No, that wasn't right. Where would someone like *Penelope* take a prospective business associate, especially one to whom she hoped to propose such an unusual merger? It didn't take much consideration. Benjamin's. Sedate, exclusive, highly private and far too bland for his tastes. It catered to high-powered businessmen intent on closing equally high-powered business deals.

Stefano shot the assistant a determined stare. "What time is her appointment at Benjamin's?"

"How did...?" Her mouth compressed. "Noon. But if you mention I told you, you'd better have a new job lined up for me. And just so you know, I don't come cheap."

"You're not going to get fired. You might even get a raise out of it." Or she would as soon as he convinced Penelope that she was better off marrying him than Cornell.

"I'll hold you to that." She checked her watch. "I'm Cindy, by the way. And if you want to arrive in time, you'd better get a move on. Ms. Wentworth doesn't believe in running late. Nor does she accept such a failing in others."

Stefano took Cindy at her word. Checking his watch as he left Crabbe and Associates he realized he had a scant ten minutes to make it to the restaurant. Fate proved to be in a good mood. A cab pulled up to the curb the moment he lifted his arm and deposited him outside of Benjamin's at precisely one minute to noon. At twelve on the dot he approached Penelope just as she and Cornell were being led to their table.

"Sorry I'm late, *cara*," he said.

Snagging her around the waist, he snatched her away from Cornell and propelled her into his arms. This time he didn't hesitate. He kissed her. A hush descended, as though the world had paused to watch. Certainly he'd captured the attention of the people waiting for a table. Not that they concerned him for long. Something far more important held his interest.

Stefano's mouth locked over Penelope's, the fit more

perfect than he could have imagined. He'd been a fool yesterday. He'd had the opportunity to kiss her in private and he hadn't taken advantage of it. He wouldn't make that mistake again. Beneath her businesslike exterior, Penelope Wentworth was lush and potent and delectable—a woman hidden beneath the trappings of the corporate world.

For the briefest of moments she resisted, her spine arching in silent protest. But the next instant everything changed. It was as though her body recognized and accepted what her mind rejected. With the most delicate of moans she opened to accommodate him, welcoming him home. Her lips were full and soft, and she tasted of coffee and a unique sweetness he'd never encountered before. To his surprise her hands slipped around his waist beneath his suit jacket and spread across his back, pressing him close.

His response was instantaneous. He tangled his hands in her hair and tilted her head to a more accessible angle. Then he drank with undisguised demand, claiming as much as he gave in return. She kissed with a delicate urgency, her unrestrained curiosity threatening his self-control. He could sense a deeper underlying hunger, an unfulfilled need he wanted to satisfy, here and now. Unfortunately here and now was impossible. He *really* should have accepted her offer last night when he could have brought a more satisfactory conclusion to the desperate desire building between them.

He ended the kiss with notable reluctance, taking a final taste before setting her free. She emerged from his embrace delightfully breathless, her hair and suit jacket just rumpled enough to erase the crisp, professional image she'd so carefully cultivated. No one would mistake her for anything other than a woman of depth and passion and strong emotion. They certainly wouldn't associate her with the cool, logical businesswoman who'd invaded his office the day before.

No. This was a passionate, vibrant woman burning with unmistakable hunger. It was a stunning revelation. As far as Stefano was concerned, it also sealed her fate. "You're mine now," he whispered against her mouth. "Signed, sealed and delivered."

"Do we have a deal?" she whispered back.

"Conditional upon final negotiations."

"Agreed."

"Shall we finalize it with another kiss?"

She refused with a satisfactory amount of regret. "I think we'll have to forgo that pleasure since it might prove a little awkward in our current setting."

"Spoilsport."

She risked a quick glance over her shoulder. "What do we do about Cornell?"

"I need you to trust me." Stefano brushed her cheekbone with his thumb, eliciting another delicious tremor. "Follow my lead, okay?"

"It'll be a struggle," she murmured dryly. "But I'll give it a try."

"Excuse me, Penelope," Cornell interrupted. Irritation edged his voice. "Are we having lunch or not?"

She attempted to conceal her awkwardness behind a mask of brisk professionalism. "I'm sorry, Robert." She made introductions as they were shown to their table. "Have you met Stefano Salvatore?"

Cornell laughed. "It's possible. There are so many Salvatore boys it's tough keeping track." He pretended to consider. "Is this the thief?"

Stefano acknowledged the insult with a broad smile.

He held out a chair for Penelope, then took the one next to her. Peering down, he was startled to discover two of his shirt buttons had come undone. Now when had that happened? He shot Penelope a speculative glance. Perhaps his bride-to-be had responded to his kiss more enthusiastically than he'd realized.

"Here's a way you can keep it straight," he informed Cornell. He rebuttoned his shirt with nonchalant disregard, using the task to add impact to his statement. "I'm the one about to marry Nellie." A nimble-fingered Nellie, it would seem.

"Nellie?" A deep frown formed between Cornell's brows. "Who's Nellie?"

She sighed. "He means me."

It only took an instant for comprehension to dawn. The news didn't sit well. "You two are getting married?"

"As soon as possible," Stefano confirmed.

"And how do I fit into the scheme of things?"

"You don't."

Penelope stirred, uncomfortably aware that the next few minutes would prove extremely awkward. "Perhaps I should explain—"

"Oh, please. Allow me," Stefano interrupted, lounging back in his chair. "My fiancée and I were going to offer to buy you out. If you're interested, we can discuss it over lunch."

Cornell chuckled. "Buy me out? Is this some sort of joke?"

"Not at all."

"You've got a nerve, Salvatore. I'll give you that. Would you mind telling me why you think I'd be the least interested in selling? If anything, I should be making you the offer. With your current reputation, I can't see you remaining in business for much longer.''

"You're mistaken. Salvatores is allowing you the opportunity to bow out gracefully while you still can." Stefano's expression iced over. "Before we go public as the new owner of Janus Corp."

"What the hell's the meaning of this?" He turned an infuriated gaze on Penelope. "You said you had something I might be interested in acquiring. You didn't say anything about buying me out."

She impressed Stefano by smiling blandly. "Oops."

"I don't know what game the two of you are playing, but you're making a mistake." He shoved back his chair and stood. "I don't play well with others."

"I've heard that about you," Stefano murmured.

Cornell planted his hands on the table and leaned close. "You're both going to regret this. No one plays me for a fool." His pale gaze switched to Stefano. "Janus Corp isn't yours yet, Salvatore. And even if you do end up acquiring it, I'll see that you don't benefit."

Stefano slowly rose, his height enough of an intimidation to cause the other man to draw back. "Give me an excuse. You think I want to buy you out?" The sound of his laugh sent a shiver of reaction coursing down Penelope's spine. "I want to see you pay for what you've done to my family."

"Your Salvatore charm is failing you," Cornell snarled. "That's the second time I've seen it happen. First with Kate Bennett and now here. What do you say to my making it three for three?" He snagged one of Penelope's curls. "How about it, *Nellie?* Dump Salvatore and back me instead. I guarantee you'll come out a winner."

"Take your hand off her."

The deeply accented order came as the softest of rumbles. For some reason, it made the demand all the more lethal—the male of the species staking his claim as clearly as though he'd howled it from a mountaintop. The elemental current carried, causing conversations to ebb and heads to turn. Silence reigned for an endless moment, the only sound the ragged give-and-take of Cornell's breath. Slowly his hand dropped from Penelope and he stepped away.

"This isn't over, Salvatore."

Stefano bared his teeth in a ferocious parody of a smile. "I hoped you'd say that."

There was a certain lack of dignity in a man trying to look casual as he turned tail and ran. Not that Cornell ran. His pace remained sedate. But no one could doubt that he'd been forced to back down before a more dominant male. Stefano grinned at the sight. He'd savor the memory for a long time to come. Too bad his brothers hadn't been able to witness it, as well.

"You're enjoying this," Penelope suddenly announced. There was no mistaking her indignation.

"You have no idea."

"Well, I won't stand for it. You said I should trust you. You said nothing about fighting over me like a feral dog." She rose and faced him. The full, sweet mouth he'd taken such pleasure in exploring formed an ominous line. "I see I'll have to take charge. Let's go, Stefano. We'll continue this meeting at my office where we can hash this matter out in private."

"Sit down, Nellie."

"You can't order me around like you did Cornell." They were still the center of attention, now even more so than before, and hot color swept across her cheekbones. "I won't stand for it."

He didn't raise his voice, but the intonation held the same ruthless intent as when he'd laid claim to her in front of Cornell. "I said… Sit. Down."

She leaned toward him until they were nearly nose to nose. Her eyes flashed more brilliantly than the golden rims of her glasses. "Listen up, Salvatore, and listen well."

The fact that she stood her ground pleased him. Most women wouldn't have dared, not after the scene with Cornell. It suggested that their marriage would match strength with strength. And the kiss they'd exchanged suggested they'd also match passion with passion. He folded his arms across his chest. "I'm listening."

"I'll sit down again since it's apparent you're not willing to return to my office. But that doesn't mean you've won. You got that? I don't take orders from anyone, no matter how well they snarl and growl."

He lifted an eyebrow at that. "You think I snarl and growl well?"

"Exceedingly well."

"Got it." He waited a beat before asking, "Mind telling me why you've decided to stay?"

"Because I'm hungry. I like the food at Benjamin's. And it takes forever to get reservations." She resumed her seat and picked up the menu, burying her nose between the pages. "People are watching. Please sit down."

He did as she requested. "Are you staying because you don't want to cause a scene or because you want lunch?"

"After considering all the options at my disposal, I've decided lunch is the most reasonable choice available." She flipped a page. "It's also the only reason I'll admit to."

Hidden behind her menu, she missed his smile, one he suspected was edged with tenderness. He was beginning to find his bride-to-be downright irresistible. "That's what I thought."

"You two know each other, don't you? You and Cornell." She peeked at him over the top of the menu, a scowl lining her brow. "I mean, on more than a business footing."

He didn't pretend to misunderstand. "We've run up against each other once or twice."

"So I gathered from what you said about him last night. But there's more to it than that, isn't there? There's real history between you." The menu lowered another inch. "Why didn't you tell me?"

"Because it has nothing to do with you."

She made a show of closing the menu, though she still clutched it close. "You mean it *had* nothing to do with me. 'Had' being the operative word. As your future wife, I deserve to know the truth."

"If you were going to be a real wife, I might agree," he retorted evenly. "As a temporary business partner, it's none of your concern."

"It has to do with a woman, doesn't it?" she guessed. "Your ex-fiancée, perhaps?"

"Try a bread stick."

"What did he do? Date her after she left you? Encourage her to leave?"

"You're not going to give up until I answer your questions, are you?"

"I'm persistent."

He shook his head. "I'd say nosy was a bit more accurate."

"Determined."

"Stubborn."

"That's a matter of perspective," she retorted, brushing aside the criticism. "Tell me the truth. Was he the reason your engagement failed? Or did he come along after the fact."

"Oh, he preceded the fact."

"That was why you warned me about him, because you were afraid he'd pull the same tricks with me that he did with her." Her lush mouth tilted into a lopsided smile and her deep, sultry laughter rang free. "That's really sweet of you."

He leaned toward her and plucked the menu from her hands. "I hate to destroy your illusions, *cara,* but I'm not being sweet. We've agreed on a business deal, remember?"

Her smile dimmed. "Of course I remember."

"You had the choice of either me or Cornell." He caught her chin in his palm, forcing her bewitching gaze to fix on him. "You've made your choice and now you're going to stick to it. I intend to see to that."

A hint of anger stirred in her expression. "I've never gone back on a deal in my life."

"So my investigator said. That's one of the reasons I'm sitting here."

"You have trust issues," she accused. "You expect me to trust you, but you can't trust me."

"Got it in one."

"Wait a minute… You also said investigator."

He smiled blandly. "I hope you'll understand my need to play it safe, considering my trust issues."

"I think we understand each other perfectly. You were burned by your fiancée and Cornell and now you don't trust anyone."

"Wrong," he instantly denied. "It's Cornell I don't trust. He's ruthless. And now that he knows my plans, he'll do anything—no matter how unethical—to stop me. I want you to go into this relationship with your eyes wide-open. You're not going to back out of your marriage proposition. It's too late now."

"I have no intention of backing out."

"Good. Then there's only one last detail we need to discuss."

"What is it?"

His hand slid slowly from her chin, leaving behind a path of fire. "The conditions of our marriage."

CHAPTER FIVE

PENELOPE waited until the waiter had taken their order and left before continuing the conversation. "I assume you have terms you want me to agree to?"

"A few."

Despite the volatile nature of the conversation, she felt comfortable with this part of the discussion. Business came naturally to her. She had no problem discussing contractual options and conditions and negotiating a deal. Anything that avoided the emotional aspects of marriage sat well with her. Besides, after what she'd learned about Stefano and his trust issues, avoiding those aspects struck her as a wise move.

"Name them."

"Obviously I require free and clear title to Janus Corporation at the rock-bottom price you referred to when we first met."

"Done."

"You're to live in my home for the duration of the marriage."

Uh-oh. She didn't like the sound of that. The waiter arrived with the bottle of wine Stefano had ordered and she suffered through the prolonged ritual of the opening and tasting before she had the opportunity to question his latest demand. "Why? Why do I have to live with you?"

"How's the wine?"

"I'm sure it's fine." She took a hasty sip to prove her point. The taste exploded on her tongue, catching her by surprise. The distinctive flavor filled her mouth, rich and full-bodied, and as delicious to the senses as Stefano's accent. "Oh, *my*. This is incredible. Very unusual."

"We import the label from Italy."

"I can see why. I rarely drink wine at lunch, but I'm willing to make an exception for this."

"Let me guess. Wine doesn't mix well with business, right?"

"Not at all."

"Now why doesn't that surprise me?"

She grinned, taking his teasing with good grace. "Oh, but it gets better. I'm also trained to ignore pure physical pleasures since they tend to be a distraction, too."

Humor gleamed in his eyes, along with an alarming spark of determination—determination that warned he planned to change all that in the near future. "Quite right. We can't allow ourselves to become distracted by such disruptive impulses."

"No, we can't." She responded to his amusement with a quick grin. "Hasn't anyone explained how this works? Food is to fuel the body, drink to quench thirst, clothes for protection, warmth and custom." A laugh broke loose. "At least, that's what I try to tell myself."

"A conclusion reached after due thought and consideration, no doubt based on pure rationality, deductive reasoning and prolonged intellectual analysis."

"Don't forget experience. If that's taught me anything, it's to never allow emotion to eclipse reason. I shudder just thinking about it." She took another, slower sip of wine, fully savoring the taste and sensation. "But perhaps I've been a little too practical."

"I think we can consider that a given." He held up the glass so the deep ruby color shimmered in the overhead light. "It's a nice little wine, though I admit I'm prejudiced. The vineyard is owned by Salvatore relatives. My father's visiting them as we speak."

"A popular brand, I assume?"

"Very." He returned the glass to the table and captured her hand in his. Caught within his hold, her fingers appeared tiny in comparison, fine-boned and frighteningly fragile versus his, which were long and capable and powerful. "I want you to live with me, Nellie, because I intend our marriage to look as normal as possible."

"Back to the practical?" she questioned wistfully. Of the two of them, it would seem Stefano was having an easier time staying focused on business. A shame. She'd been taking such pleasure in forgetting a few of those hard-won lessons Loren had drummed into her over the years.

"It won't last long, I promise. It's not my style."

"In that case, I can be magnanimous." She swept a hand through the air. "Proceed."

For an instant she thought he'd drop the wedding negotiations. But then he continued. "Considering the haste of the ceremony, I suspect there will be a lot of talk. I'd rather not provide any more than necessary."

"Talk." Why hadn't she thought of that? Naturally there'd be gossip about their actions. They were both too well-known in the business community to avoid it. And no doubt the current stain on Salvatores' reputation would add fuel to the discussion. "I don't suppose there's any way of avoiding a certain amount of talk about our personal affairs. But it shouldn't last long."

"Particularly once they realize you're not pregnant."

Penelope reached for her wineglass with an unsteady hand. "Pregnant?"

"That's the first assumption people will make. Care to take a wild stab at what their next guess will be?"

She didn't wait for Stefano to refill her glass. She helped herself. "That we're madly, passionately in love?"

She didn't know where the words came from, but had the uneasy suspicion they escaped from some deep, closely guarded part of herself. Worse, she was willing to bet her comment resulted from wishful thinking rather than a more palatable excuse—like the wine she'd been drinking. Something about Stefano and the intimate aspects of their conversation had unlocked the forbidden. And once out in the open, she feared she'd have the very devil of a time locking those emotions away again.

"Whether or not people believe we're in love will depend on how we act toward each other. No, the second round of gossip will start up as soon as they discover that you're in control of Crabbe and Associates. I assume the particulars of your parents' will aren't general knowledge?"

"No, they're not."

"Once you officially take over, people will suspect you married in order to oust your uncle, particularly when news leaks that Salvatores has purchased Janus Corp." He paused a beat before adding, "And it will be the truth, won't it?"

"Yes," she whispered. "There are reasons—"

"Which brings me to my third condition."

She didn't need him to spell it out. There wasn't a doubt in her mind what he wanted for his third condition—an explanation for her actions. "Don't make it a condition, Stefano. I can't tell you why I'm doing this. Not yet. Not until we're safely married."

"Why?"

"It's confidential. If I explained further it could put Crabbe and Associates at risk. And I won't do that. I can't. My business interests have to come first."

"You'd allow others to suspect you don't have any confidence in your uncle's abilities?"

She stared in alarm. "What do you mean?"

The waiter appeared with their lunch and Penelope waited impatiently while he unloaded his tray. Her grilled chicken salad—dressing on the side—didn't look nearly as tempting as Stefano's blackened tiger prawns and scallops. To her astonishment, he took one look at her expression and slipped a portion of his meal from his plate to hers.

"What are you doing?"

"What do you think? I'm giving you what you really want."

"If I'd wanted prawns, I'd have ordered them."

The darkness of his gaze was far too penetrating for comfort. "Somehow I doubt that. You strike me as someone who makes her choices based on everything *except* personal desire. You've practically said as much." He forked a succulent morsel of shrimp and held it to her lips. "Let go, cara. Enjoy yourself."

Giving in to temptation would set a bad precedent, especially when it was Stefano doing the tempting. But she couldn't resist. She took the forbidden bite and sighed, savoring the flavor. The prawn tasted as good as it smelled, particularly accentuated with another sip of wine. "Red wine and seafood aren't supposed to go together."

"Are you enjoying the wine?"

"Yes."

"And the seafood?"

"Very much."

"Then don't analyze what you should do or what's supposed to work. Simply appreciate the unexpected pleasure." He waited until she'd finished her meal before resuming business. "About your uncle..."

She looked up in abject guilt. How could she have forgotten their discussion? She'd never done that before meeting Stefano. And yet with him, it had become all too regular an occurrence. "Yes, of course. You were going to tell me how our marriage would adversely affect my uncle."

"If there's any suspicion that you're marrying in order to take over Crabbe and Associates, it will put your uncle in a very awkward position. Your board will assume it's a vote of no-confidence, as will the general public."

"I won't let anything hurt my uncle."

Stefano leaned forward and lowered his voice. "*You're* going to hurt him. Have you discussed your marriage plans with him?"

How could she? Not that she could explain that to Stefano. "No, I haven't discussed them."

"Don't you think walking into the next board meeting and assuming charge will humiliate him?"

She hadn't thought of that and should have. It was a logical progression. Of course, she hadn't planned to make the changeover in front of the board, though the results could very well be the same. Why was nothing about this easy? Perhaps because she'd been forced to make this decision without the opportunity to plan a strategy. "What do you suggest?" she asked tightly.

"We don't have a lot of time to spare because of Cornell, but I suggest we spend the next few weeks creating a whirlwind romance. Let people think we're falling in love."

"Is that really necessary?"

"It's not just Loren I'm considering. I have my father to worry about, too. Dom will be much more accepting of our marriage if he believes love prompted it, rather than business." He allowed her to mull that over before continuing. "According to my investigator, you have a birthday in a few weeks. It will provide the perfect opportunity to fly to Vegas or Reno and have an impromptu wedding. It will cause talk, but it won't throw suspicion on your motives or on your uncle's abilities. People will think you finally decided to cut loose and took it to extreme measures."

That made sense, despite her reluctance to waste the next few weeks faking a romance. If it helped Uncle Loren save face and satisfied Stefano's father, she wouldn't object. "Okay. I'll agree to that condition, as well. Anything else?"

"We'd better discuss the duration of the marriage."

"It doesn't have to last long at all."

"Yes, it does."

"Stefano—"

"If we marry and divorce in a few short months, we'll both end up looking like fools. That won't help either of our careers. Is there any reason the marriage can't last a while?"

"What if we meet someone else?"

She wished he'd stop staring at her as though he could see straight through to her soul. "Is that likely?" he asked roughly.

His tone had acquired far too possessive a quality and she fought against it with the most outrageous lie she could manage. "I could meet someone tomorrow."

He didn't take the bait. "Then I suggest you forget about marrying me and wait until you find that someone."

"Darn it, Stefano! You know I have no interest in marrying you or anyone else. If it weren't for—" She broke off, painfully aware that she'd almost given herself away. She thrust the wineglass to a safe distance, wishing she could do the same with Stefano. Both caused ungovernable reactions, something she couldn't afford right now. "If it weren't for certain unforeseen events, I wouldn't be marrying now."

"You flatter me, *cara*," he murmured in a dry tone.

She fought for control. "I apologize, Stefano. That was rude." If she didn't move this conversation along, there might not be a marriage to negotiate. The way she was going, she was likely to insult her way out of it. "You want to live together? Fine. You think the marriage should last a while? I'll agree to that, too. Now I have a question for you. Will we have to live together the entire time?"

"It's possible. I suggest we remain flexible on that point." A slight smile eased the harshness around his mouth. "Do you know how to do flexible?"

"I'll give it a stab." The waiter removed their plates. Before Penelope could protest, he placed a delicious-looking chocolate-and-raspberry cheesecake in front of her. "I couldn't possibly eat this."

"Not part of today's scheduled food intake?" Stefano jibbed.

She snatched up her fork and glared at him. Demolishing the decadent dessert, she acknowledged that he knew precisely which buttons to push to get her to do as he wished. She stewed over that distressing fact as she scraped the last smidgeon of chocolate from her plate.

"I have a condition of my own," she announced.

"And what's that?"

She adjusted her glasses with a determined air. "I want it clearly understood that I'll be in charge of our marriage. I make the decisions. I call the shots. I choose what we do and when we do it."

"And my role?"

She smiled grimly. "You get to obey."

"What happens if I don't agree to this rather interesting condition?"

"I'll go pay a visit to Mr. Cornell and see if he won't be more willing," she answered promptly.

It was the most outrageous bluff she'd ever attempted and she suspected he knew it. Even so, she refused to back down, just as she refused to spend the next weeks and months having her buttons pushed by Stefano Salvatore. She wasn't about to gain her independence on one front only to lose it on another.

An odd smile tugged at the corners of his mouth. "You propose an interesting condition, *cara*."

The return of his accent should have warned her. "Then you agree?"

"This is your only condition? You're sure it's what you want? *All* you want?"

"I'm positive," she announced with more bravado than honesty.

"Then that's what you will have." He leaned across the table to seal his promise with far too brief a kiss. "I'll see to it personally."

This had to stop, Stefano told himself as he hailed a cab. He didn't want a real relationship with Penelope. Ever since Kate Bennett he'd been off both women and commitment. Oh, not permanently. He wasn't a total fool. One day the right woman would come along.

But she wasn't Penelope Wentworth.

To continue to play the sort of games he had over lunch could only lead one place—to total disaster. What if he began to care about her? What if she came to care about him? One of them was guaranteed a world of hurt. He could handle it. But what about Penelope?

Oh, she'd rationalize away the heartache. She'd find some logical explanation for why their relationship hadn't worked. But inside, deep inside where logic had no place and hurt left bruising fingerprints on fragile emotions, she'd change. And it wouldn't be for the better.

No. If he were smart, he'd keep their association as unemotional and painless as possible. He'd make certain she understood their marriage would remain a business proposition, no more. That way they'd both remain safe.

That way there'd be no harm, no foul.

This had to stop, Penelope told herself as she exited the cab outside Crabbe and Associates. She didn't want a real relationship with Stefano, certainly not the type of marriage he seemed to be insisting upon. It sounded far too risky. Someday, maybe. After all, she wasn't a total fool. One day the right man would come along.

But he wasn't Stefano Salvatore.

To continue to play the sort of games she had over lunch could only lead one place—to total disaster. What if he began to care about her? What if she came to care about him? One of them was guaranteed a world of hurt. She could handle it. But what about Stefano?

Oh, he'd deal with the heartache. He had with Kate Bennett. But it would consume some of the passionate spark that illuminated his soul. It would eat away at the charm and the grace and the protective generosity she found so attractive. It would change him. And it wouldn't be for the better.

No. If she were smart, she'd keep their association as unemotional and painless as possible. She'd make certain he understood their marriage would remain a business proposition, no more. That way they'd both remain safe.

That way there'd be no harm, no foul.

Stefano held the receiver to his ear with an uplifted shoulder and gazed out of his office window. "I don't understand the problem." He leaned back in his chair and silently counted the windows fronting Crabbe and Associates until he reached the corner office Penelope occupied. Was she sitting at her desk, staring out the window and counting office windows, too? "You agreed that we'd have a whirlwind romance."

Her voice acquired an odd, high-pitched intonation. "A whirlwind romance involves flowers or candy. The occasional dinner date. It doesn't involve—" She gulped air. "It doesn't involve *you know what*."

"I see." He grinned. "People were around when you opened the box, weren't they?"

"Yes, people were around!" He could practically hear her gnash her teeth. "There were three presidents from three different firms sitting in my office when your gift arrived. I assumed from the shape of the box that it was chocolates. I thought opening your gift would be an excellent way to let people know we were romantically involved."

"You must have realized it was too light for chocolates."

"No, I did not realize it was too light."

He straightened in his seat, a frown tugging at his

brow. "And why is that, *cara?* Hasn't anyone ever sent you chocolates?"

"We're getting off the point."

A painful vulnerability had crept into her voice, a vulnerability he'd have given anything to ease. "You'll excuse me if I say that's precisely the point. Are all the men you've ever known blind? Or just stupid?"

He could sense her struggle for composure and an image formed in his mind, one he'd seen many times since meeting her. At the first sign of opposition, she'd straighten her glasses and lift her chin. The overhead lights would catch in her hair, softening the tawny streaks and igniting the gold. If he'd been there with her, she'd have fixed him with gleaming eyes filled with determination. And then she'd argue with unending logical precision.

When they'd first met, her cool, calm facade had been sufficient to fool him. But no longer. A woman's sensitivity lurked beneath the surface. And with it burned an emotional warmth and irresistible allure. Where most saw the practical businesswoman, he saw a delicious feminine mystique, one that tempted him past endurance. Stefano's mouth twisted.

So much for keeping a professional distance.

"I haven't called in order to discuss my past relationships," she stated. "Have you any idea of the reaction when I opened your gift?"

He reluctantly allowed the conversation to return to the subject at hand. "I know how I would have reacted. What did your visitors do?"

"They— Never mind what they did! Suffice to say that the reaction was all you could have wished. There's no doubt in anyone's mind that the two of us are conducting a torrid affair."

"Perfect."

"It is *not* perfect. By any chance, do you recall agreeing to my being in charge of our relationship?"

"No."

He'd thrown her with that one. "What do you mean, no? My one condition to this proposition was—"

"—was that you'd be in charge of our marriage. I don't believe we're married, yet."

Her ragged breathing blasted through the receiver. "Stefano?"

"Yes, *cara?*"

"Are you in your office?"

"Sitting at my desk, staring out the window."

"Staring at the window to my office?"

"As a matter of fact, I am. For some reason, I do that a lot these days."

"Stay right where you are. Don't move a muscle until I get there. Is that clear?"

"As clear as my gift."

"It was *sheer*, not *clear!*" With that, she slammed the phone down.

Stefano smiled as he punched the button to disconnect his portable phone and tossed it onto the desk. Interesting. It would seem his bride-to-be was in a bit of a snit. Got her impeccable feathers all in a ruffle. His smile grew to a grin. He looked forward to seeing this side of her, assuming she remained ruffled for the few minutes it took to walk from her building to his.

He didn't have long to wait. Blatantly disobeying her "order," he left his office and headed toward the elevators. Halfway there, he heard the warning ping of an arriving car. Something in the strident sound suggested it might be Penelope.

It was.

"Stefano Salvatore, I told you not to move." He heard her voice even before he could see her.

"Hello, Penelope."

Stefano released his breath in a long sigh. Damn. This was definitely not a good sign. If he was here, and she was there, then her opening salvo could only have been directed toward one other person. He arrived in time to see Penelope clutching a fistful of Marco's jacket in one hand and waving her index finger beneath his nose with the other. At the opposite end of the hallway, Hanna was bearing down on Penelope. Stefano bit off an expletive and broke into a jog. It would appear a collision was inevitable.

"Don't you 'hello, Penelope' me!" She stopped waving her finger and started poking Marco's chest with it. "I want you to explain why you sent me that underwear. What in the world were you thinking?"

"Er—"

Hanna arrived first. Linking arms with Marco, she gently removed Penelope's fist from her husband's suit jacket and smoothed the offending wrinkles. "Yes, do explain yourself, Marco," she encouraged sweetly. "I'd also like to hear why my husband is sending intimate apparel to a woman other than his wife."

"Marco?" Penelope broke off midjab. "You're... you're *Marco?*"

"Afraid so. My brother is over there." He pointed toward Stefano. "He's the one with the really furious expression."

She flinched. "Uh-oh."

Time to step in. "I'll handle this, if you don't mind," Stefano said. He scooped up his future wife before she had a chance to open her mouth again. Not that such an unusual state of affairs lasted for long.

"There's a logical explanation for this," she began, squirming in his arms.

He stilled her restless movements by tightening his hold. Her breath escaped in a startled rush and she sank into his embrace, her entire body becoming soft and pliable and lushly feminine. His mouth tightened in frustration. Did she even realize how instinctively she responded to him? Couldn't she use that response to tell him from his brother?

"A logical explanation." He repeated the words in a clipped tone, finding himself heartily sick of the phrase. "It doesn't surprise me that you think so. Unfortunately you're not going to be able to logic your way clear of this situation. I should also warn you that your logic has the uncanny knack of annoying the hell out of me. Particularly when you're dead wrong."

"Stefano—"

"Not now."

Something in his voice stopped her cold. The minute he'd gained his office and closeted them behind a locked door, he released her. She stumbled into the room, straightening first her suit jacket, then her glasses and finally her hair. Unruffling her ruffles, no doubt. Planting his back against the solid oak door, he deliberately remained silent, afraid if he opened his mouth he'd be unable to halt the fierce torrent of words. Then he waited.

Penelope cleared her throat. "Under the circumstances, complaining about your gift loses its punch at this juncture."

"You thought Marco was me." The words rumbled across the room.

Her eyes widened at the sound. "Well, yes—"

"*Again.*" The rumble grew louder.

Lightning flashed in her eyes in response. "You say that as though it were deliberate. In case you've forgotten, you two look alike. It's hard to tell the difference."

"You'll have a hard time convincing everyone we're madly in love if you keep confusing the two of us."

"Perhaps name tags?"

"I assume that's an attempt at humor?" He straightened away from the door, aware that this clash had been inevitable, brewing between them from the start.

Her hand whipped upward to adjust her glasses once more. Other than that single telling gesture, she managed to retain her composure. It impressed him no end. It also made him all the more determined to shake her icy calm and expose the passion sparking beneath.

"Have you noticed that your accent is back?" she announced.

"Does it make you nervous?"

"Very." A hint of irritation broke through, blazing across her face for a brief instant—Nellie eclipsing Penelope. "I assume the accent is a result of your being upset."

"A distinct possibility."

"I came here to discuss your present, in case you've forgotten and I don't intend to get sidetracked."

The tension built, crackling between them with all the fury and energy of a burgeoning electrical storm. All it needed was a single spark to set off the chain reaction. "Oh, we're going to get sidetracked. Count on it."

"Would it help if I apologize? I really did mistake Marco for you."

"As I've already explained, that doesn't make me feel better. You won't be able to convince people that we're serious if you continue confusing me with my brother."

"Do you have any suggestions?"

"One." He slowly approached, not in the least surprised when she chose to stand her ground. Penelope was not a woman easily intimidated. Not even when confronted with an infuriated husband-to-be. He didn't stop until they stood inches apart. Plucking her glasses from the tip of her nose, he tossed them to the nearby couch. "I suggest you find a way to tell us apart other than name tags."

Her chin came up in a familiar motion and her eyes turned molten. "Like I said…" Defiance ripped through her voice—agitating, inciting, arousing. "Do you have any suggestions?"

"How about this one."

Wrapping a hand around her nape, Stefano tugged her into his arms. He only gave her enough time to snatch a quick, hungry breath before covering her mouth with his. It was the spark he'd been waiting for.

And from that single spark came the inevitable explosion.

CHAPTER SIX

STEFANO consumed Penelope's mouth, the storm breaking over them, roaring to greedy life. It was a ferocious clashing of the most raw and fundamental of the elements. Hard. Demanding. Primitive. Desperate. He cupped her face, tilting her head back to a more advantageous angle. She groaned softly and he inhaled the needy sound, determined to fulfill each and every desire.

Their mouths joined and parted. Once. Twice. Then they melded, fusing together with a perfection he'd never known before. Her arms closed around him, circling his waist. The kneading pressure of her fingernails encouraged him to lock her tighter into his embrace. Tripping backward, he thudded against the office door, pulling her with him. He used the solid oak to brace them, to support limbs that had grown weak with want. Then his hands drifted downward, branding her from the soft roundness of her breast to the womanly flare of her hip to the most intimate of spots, a place that trembled beneath his touch.

It wasn't enough. He thrust a thigh between her legs and filled his hands with her deliciously rounded bottom, lifting her closer still. Her skirt rode upward, baring the tops of her stockings, as well as her garter. She was beautiful in her passion. With her head tipped back and waves of gold-streaked hair cascading over her shoulders, her exposed throat tempted him beyond endurance. He kissed the sweet length from her chin to the vulnerable hollow at the base of her neck. Fumbling with the buttons of her ivory suit jacket, he ripped it off her shoulders and tossed it aside. It fell in a pale crumpled heap near the couch, a white flag of surrender.

"Show me how you feel, Nellie. Tell me what you're thinking."

"I think I was wrong." The words came in soft, urgent gasps.

"Wrong? Wrong about what?"

"You are charming. In fact you're downright bewitching."

He chuckled, his breath a warm balm across her skin. "No, *cara*. You're the one who's bewitching me. You put your spell on me the first time I looked into your eyes."

Penelope stared in amazement. He found her bewitching? No one had ever described her that way before. In fact, it was probably the very last word they'd use to describe her. Of course, no one had ever kissed her the way Stefano had. It was a kiss that defied logic and reason and even analysis. It made no sense at all, and yet it felt so right.

"Please, Stefano." Unable to resist, she reached upward. Tangling her fingers in his dark hair, she urged his mouth back down to hers. "One last kiss."

"You're fooling yourself if you think this will be the last."

"We'll discuss it. Later."

"Much later."

Muttering an Italian endearment, he caught her lower lip between his teeth and tugged. Her control vanished and she surged against him. Their tongues tangled, hot and driven, dueling for supremacy. It was a battle neither of them could win, not when the very word implied a single victor, one overcoming the other. She wouldn't find completion that way. He must have reached the same conclusion, for the tenor of the war they waged changed. The instant the battle turned to a mating dance, Penelope knew she was in trouble.

There was only one place this could lead and she wasn't ready for that.

"Stefano, please," she whispered. "We have to stop."

He reluctantly lifted his head. "The door's bolted. No one will disturb us."

"This isn't what we want."

"Yes, *cara*. I'm afraid it is."

"Okay. Then it's not what we *should* want. Nor is it the point of the exercise."

"Exercise?" He lifted a questioning eyebrow, regret edging his words. "I gather Penelope has returned."

"'Fraid so."

He released her, restoring her clothing to a semblance of order with a few deft tugs. It was almost as intimate a touch as his kiss. "Let's hope this little 'exercise' was successful and you'll now be able to tell me apart from my brother."

Penelope ran her tongue across her swollen lower lip. She could still taste him and an irresistible warmth pooled in the pit of her stomach. This would never do! She couldn't allow him to affect her this way. "It's a start."

Far more than a start, if she were honest. Surely she wouldn't get them confused again. Because Stefano was right. If she kept mistaking the Salvatore brothers, she'd undermine all the good they were trying to accomplish. Although she hadn't initially seen the benefit in pretending a romance, Stefano had made a valid point. Her uncle would be devastated by her actions if she married and immediately afterward forced a takeover. A love affair, however, allowed him to save face.

"Is that the only reason you kissed me the way you did?" he demanded. "As an exercise to tell me from my brother? Somehow I don't think so. I think you want more than that. I know I do."

She shook her head, panic overriding every other emotion. "That's not possible. It's not what we agreed to."

"What if I've changed my mind?" he pressed. "You've been warned that I'm not a man who honors his word."

She dismissed the last part of his statement with a wave of her hand. But the first part intrigued her. "Have you changed your mind?"

He smiled in a way that made her feel as though she were free-falling without a parachute. Unfortunately, no parachute meant an eventual crash to earth. "Be honest, Nellie. Do you think we can live with each other for months on end and not take this a step further?"

The crash had come far sooner than she'd expected. "So we should make love because it's inevitable?"

"No. We should make love because it's what we both want."

She forced herself to step well clear of his arms and employ rational thought rather than untidy emotions. "I never said I wanted to make love with you. We kissed. It was...nice. End of story."

"Nice?"

Perhaps she shouldn't have dismissed those moments in his arms with such callous disregard. It seemed to have had the unfortunate result of rousing his anger again. She sighed. Men were such prickly creatures. "All right, fine. It was better than nice. You're quite good at it. But I don't see any point in turning it into a major life event. I'm sure you've kissed plenty of women without feeling the need to take them to bed." She started to adjust her glasses and suddenly realized they weren't there. "Or am I mistaken?"

"You're not mistaken."

Before she could guess his intent, he caught her hand and tugged, returning her to his arms. Their bodies collided, reigniting tiny explosions of desire. It had to be a chemical reaction. There couldn't be any other reasonable explanation. Something about Stefano's body chemistry—pheromones or his scent or the natural combustion of skin abrading skin—affected her in ways she couldn't explain. It stirred a longing she'd never experienced before, driving her to respond on an elemental level. It was primitive and desperate and irrational.

It was also totally irresistible.

She attempted to back away, but he followed, every movement one of unspoken seduction and innate grace. She bumped against the arm of the couch and lost her footing. He caught her before she could fall, twisting so that he was the one who landed on the couch cushions with Penelope on top of him.

"Give yourself to me, Nellie."

"I can't. We can't."

His gaze never left hers, his eyes filled with an enticing combination of hunger and patience. "Give yourself to me."

She silenced him the only way she knew how. She cupped his face, the softness of her palms abraded by the faintest rasping burn from his jawline. Heaven help her, but he was gorgeous. Tension had drawn the skin taut across his cheekbones and driven brackets alongside his mouth, emphasizing the fullness of his lips. Long, thick lashes framed midnight-black eyes—eyes that had witnessed both intense joy and darkest sorrow and chose to reflect back the joy.

"What will you do when you have me?" she whispered.

"Cherish you."

A tremor shook her at the undeniable sincerity in his words. She couldn't listen to any more, no matter how much his promise made her soul sing. She found his mouth with unerring accuracy, pleading without words, taking a fleeting rapture in the momentary joining. She felt his hands at her blouse, felt the buttons give way one by one. She deepened the kiss, shutting out the voice of reason, pushing aside duty and responsibility and all rational thought.

Instead she allowed herself to simply feel.

His lips flirted with hers, his tongue wickedly playful. She wanted to laugh and cry and moan all at the same time. He bewildered her, delighted her, aroused her. But most of all he stirred those sensations she craved, coaxing them forth from deep within and then bestowing them on her in return. Her blouse fell open and he tugged down the top edge of her bra, releasing her breasts. They filled his hands, the tips burgeoning within his palms. Faint calluses abraded the sensitive nipples and she groaned at the sensation. He lifted her higher and her groan became a gasp as he took a furled tip into his mouth, catching it with his teeth.

"Stefano!"

"Yes, *cara*. Say my name. Inhale me. Taste me. Take me inside of you. I want to imprint myself on you so you'll never confuse me with anyone else."

The soft curls of her hair spilled across his face and

shoulders in an erotic caress. "I couldn't. Not after this."

"I'm going to make sure of it."

He reached down and cupped her thighs, parting them. She squirmed, cradling the ridge of his desire against the most feminine part of her. His hands swept relentlessly upward, tracing the top edge of her stockings and the flimsy straps that held them in place. And then he explored further still. His fingers found the edge of her panties and slipped beneath to stroke the moist, heated core within. Her breath burst from her lungs in a muted shriek.

"No more," she cried, her head dropping to his chest. His heart pounded beneath her cheek. "I can't take any more."

"I know, *cara*. I feel the same way."

She closed her eyes tight, fighting for breath. "So I noticed."

He lifted her chin, forcing her to look at him. "Now tell me this is nothing more than nice. Tell me how our marriage will remain a passionless contract. You might hate the idea, but what happens between us *is* inevitable. It was decided from the moment you walked in this office and propositioned me. Fight it, *cara*. Fight if it will make you feel better. But the surrender will come. And not all your logic or determination will change that."

She didn't dare believe him. "You're mistaken. I'm not controlled by my emotions."

To her frustration, he merely smiled. "Keep telling yourself that, Nellie."

"I don't need to tell myself anything. It's you who needs to understand."

If she didn't leave now, she'd give in to those emotions she'd denied so vehemently. She wriggled free of his hold and stood. Gasping at the state of her clothing, she tugged first at her bra, then her skirt and finally re-worked the buttons to her blouse. Never before had she come so undone. How had Stefano managed it? Clearly he was as dangerous to her equilibrium as he was to her clothes.

She glanced over her shoulder, throwing him a look of sheer defiance. "This discussion is at an end, Mr. Salvatore."

"Postponed, Ms. Wentworth. Consider it postponed." He shifted, wincing as he did so. "I hate to tell you this, but using my couch might have been a mistake."

"Aside from the obvious reason, you mean?"

Amusement lit his gaze. "If the obvious reason is making love to you, then yes. Aside from that."

"Why? What's wrong?"

He sat up and felt behind him, plucking free a man-gled piece of gold wire and glass. "Damn. I'm sorry, Nellie. I forgot I tossed your glasses onto the couch."

"Forget it. At least the glass didn't break. And it'll serve as an excellent reminder of what I should be avoid-ing in the future."

She took her glasses from him and straightened the rims the best she could before perching them on the tip of her nose. If the swiftly controlled twitch of his lips was anything to go by, they must look utterly ludicrous. But they helped restore her business persona. She wel-comed the return of her control with a feeling of relief that bordered on desperation.

Stefano sat up and thrust a hand through his hair. "I suggest we discuss the present I sent since it upset you sufficiently to bring you charging over here."

"Good." How could she have forgotten? She paced

in front of him, struggling to fan the embers of her annoyance. "Excellent. About your present..."

"You didn't like it."

"It's not that—"

He rubbed his jaw. "Bad color choice, perhaps?"

"No, no. I'm quite fond of ivory. It's just—"

"I selected the wrong size." A frown creased his
brow. "Though now that I've had the opportunity
to...er...fully explore the situation, I'm pretty sure I got
the size right."

"The size is perfect!" she snapped. "And stop looking at me in that tone."

He grinned. "I'm looking at you in a certain tone?"

"Yes! You're remembering what we—" Her gaze
drifted to the couch and she fought to keep from blush-
ing. "Never mind. Just cut it out."

"If it's not the size or the color, then what's wrong?"

"It was what you chose to give me. Courting couples
send each other flowers or candy—"

"Courting couples?" He stood, thrusting his shirttails
into his trousers and fastening the buttons from his waist
upward. Then he snagged his tie from off the floor and
draped it around his collar. "How quaint."

She blinked in surprise. When had she undone his
shirt and removed his tie? Aside from a vague memory
of resting her cheek against the hard, bronzed width of
his chest, she couldn't recall. But she must have since
the evidence stood before her. "You know what I mean!
Why did you send me undergarments instead of flowers
or candy?"

"Marco gave Hanna flowers and candy. Oh, and
feathers."

He succeeded in distracting her with that one. "Feathers?"

"I didn't quite get the purpose behind them, but every time I've asked they start laughing." He worked his tie, the unexpected intimacy of such a simple act catching her off guard. "And though he achieved excellent—if unanticipated—results with his choices, I decided against following in his footsteps."

She stared at him in utter bewilderment. "Why?"

"It was another attempt to differentiate us in your mind."

"I think you're sufficiently differentiated," she murmured dryly.

"To be honest, Nellie, I considered sending you chocolate or a couple dozen roses, but decided it was too trite. Since we were anxious to move our whirlwind wedding along at a rapid pace, I chose silk and lace. That way no one would mistake the nature of our relationship."

"You're right on that account."

"So what happened when you opened my present?"

She folded her arms across her chest. It was a telling gesture. "I was so startled by what you'd sent, I dropped the box."

"Wait a minute." His eyes narrowed. "Didn't you say you had company at the time?"

"Three presidents from three different firms."

He grinned. "I'll bet that caused quite a stir."

"I don't think they could have been more surprised if I'd released a rattlesnake in their midst."

"What did you do?"

"I stood there with my mouth opening and closing for a good thirty seconds. Then I snatched everything up off the floor. Or tried to." She planted her hands on her hips. "Have you any idea how slippery silk can be?"

His grin widened. "Yes, *cara*. I'm quite familiar with how slippery silk can be. It saddens me that you aren't."

"I like cotton," she retorted defensively.

"So I've discovered." His comment didn't go over well. Nor would his next, he suspected. "We'll have to see what we can do about that."

"No, we won't. As of today you're to keep all silk and lace to yourself. Understood?"

"Kinky."

"Stefano!"

"Oh, I understand that's what you'd prefer." He crossed the room to where her suit jacket lay puddled on the floor. "But that's not what's going to happen."

She balked at his certainty. "And why not?"

He snagged the jacket and held it for her so she could slip it on. "Because we've agreed to do everything we can to convince people we're now a couple. We *were* off to a great start right up until you assaulted my brother."

"You promised to handle things my way."

"No, I didn't. I promised you could be in charge of our marriage, not our romance. Face facts, Nellie. Now that you've announced to the world that Marco's been sending you silk undies, I'm going to have to work twice as hard to convince everyone that we're serious about each other. I won't have our relationship further compromised."

"That's not a problem. Anyone who sees me now won't be in any doubt as to my feelings for you." She glanced down at herself and winced. "Just look at me."

"You look beautiful." And she did. Before him stood a passionate, vibrant woman, one moreover who'd been thoroughly savored in every sense of the word.

"You've wrinkled me," she accused.

He chuckled. "Never let it be said that a Salvatore doesn't give his all." She started to respond and he waved her silent. "Relax, *cara*. You wear wrinkles well."

"That's a matter of opinion."

His laughter died, replaced by fierce desire. "My opinion is the only one that matters."

She released her breath in an impatient sigh, but she didn't bother to argue further. "No more outrageous gifts, Stefano. We can convince people we're indulging in a torrid romance without draping my office with bras and thongs and other assorted lingerie. We can also do it without wrinkling me."

"You want traditional gifts, is that it? Fine. You've got it. But I intend to wrinkle the hell out of you on a regular basis. No only is it my duty, it's my pleasure."

She didn't trust the gleam in his eyes. He was planning something and she had a sneaking suspicion she wouldn't like whatever it was. Or maybe she'd like it too much—a far more dangerous proposition. "Perhaps you should run your ideas by me before acting on them."

He folded his arms across his chest. "I don't think so."

"It would be safer."

"Don't even go there, Nellie. I'll let you control a lot in our relationship, but be careful how far you push. You may get more than you bargained for."

"Let me guess. That's not a threat, it's a promise. Right?"

"Do you doubt it?"

He hadn't moved a muscle and yet Penelope found herself backing away. Masculine aggression had never bothered her, she'd been around it for too many years.

But something about Stefano resonated within, sparking off her most feminine facets, like light refracting off a polished gemstone. He had the power to bring her to life, to expose her—the depth and richness and clarity, as well as the flaws. He saw too much, could elicit far more than she cared to give.

Worse, she'd overlooked or ignored the sheer power of the man, both physical and intellectual. It came as a distinct shock to realize that it wasn't a force she could easily handle. She could only hope that his own self-control kept those forces in check. Because she'd already discovered how difficult they were to contain once released.

"Now that we've gotten everything straightened out, I'm going," she announced.

His eyes held her, eyes that saw too much. She took another step backward and a knowing smile cut across his face. "We *will* finish this conversation," he said. "You realize that? And when we do, it won't be in an office setting. It'll be someplace private where we won't be interrupted until we're through and I've proven my point."

She lifted her chin and lied with aplomb. "I look forward to it."

If she stayed any longer she'd lose more than she could hope to win. Turning, she left his office and walked toward the elevators, head held high. It might be a retreat, but it would be a dignified one. She stabbed the elevator button. Instantly she thought of a thousand comments she could have made. Devastating remarks and logical arguments. When she returned to her office, she'd write them all down. That way she'd be prepared next time he swept her into his arms and kissed her senseless.

She attempted to smooth a few of Stefano's wrinkles with only limited success. If only she hadn't responded on a physical level. It would have resolved everything. Darn it! She stabbed at the call button again. Where was the elevator?

"Impatient to leave?"

She swiveled and glared at Stefano. "Don't start with me. I think you've done quite enough for one day."

"Excuse me?"

"Oh, don't give me that innocent look." Perhaps in the few seconds she had available before the elevator arrived she could put a few of those arguments she'd come up with to good use. "You seem to think that all you have to do is touch me and I'll do whatever you want. Well, you're wrong and I'm going to prove it."

She marched over to him, grabbed him by the lapels of his suit jacket and yanked him downward to a reachable level. Before he had time to take charge of their latest embrace, she planted her mouth on his and kissed him for all she was worth. Then she let go and stepped back, not giving any inconvenient chemistry an opportunity to kick in. Not that it did.

She straightened her cockeyed glasses. "There. See? Nothing. Not a twinge of pleasure."

"I'm pleased to hear it," a voice gritted from behind her. "I'd be a little upset if my future bride enjoyed kissing my brother more than she enjoyed kissing me."

Oh, no! Not again. Penelope risked a quick glance over her shoulder and shuddered. Stefano did not look happy. In fact, she suspected they were about to have another "discussion" and this one would no doubt end far differently than the first. To her everlasting relief, the elevator pinged and the car doors opened. She plunged inside and stabbed at the button for the lobby.

"I have only one thing to say, Stefano Salvatore," she announced as the doors started to close.

"That's about a thousand things fewer than I have."

Her mouth slanted into a wry smile. "No doubt."

"Go on, *cara*. You're dying to tell me something. Say it."

"Thank heaven you're not a triplet."

And with that, the doors slid closed.

Penelope's gift to Stefano arrived by the end of the day.

"Aren't you going to open it?" Marco asked his brother.

Stefano studied the box suspiciously. "I'm almost afraid to."

"You think this present is her way of getting even for what you sent?"

"Oh, no question."

"Come on," Marco goaded with a grin. "Open it and let's see how bad it is."

Stefano picked up the box. It was much larger than the one he'd sent Penelope and definitely heavier. It also rattled. What had his sweet fiancée sent him? He ripped off the wrapping paper and removed the lid. Inside were a half-dozen smaller gifts, all individually wrapped. He picked up the first, a long triangular object. Peeling off the paper he uncovered a brass name plate for his desk.

Marco choked on a laugh. "Well, that's one solution. Though if she wants it to do any good, you'll have to hang it around your neck."

"This is getting ridiculous," Stefano bit out. "How on earth am I going to convince anyone we're in love if she keeps mistaking us? And stop laughing! She kissed you thinking it was me. That's not even a little funny."

Marco sighed. "It was just a quick one. It barely even qualified as an actual kiss. And she said herself—she didn't feel a thing."

"That's supposed to make me any happier?"

"It could have been worse. What if she'd enjoyed it?"

"I suspect Hanna would have had something to say about it."

"Oh, Hanna has plenty to say. None of it polite enough for me to repeat." Marco peered into the box. "What else did Penelope send?"

Stefano removed the next box and ripped it open. Inside he found a gold key ring with his name spelled out. His anger faded, replaced by amusement. The next package contained a tie clip, the one after that a pen, then a briefcase, followed by a pair of suspenders. Every last one was embossed with his name in huge, gold lettering.

He began to chuckle. "It would seem Nellie has a sense of humor." It pleased him no end. He didn't think he could deal with a woman without one. He'd discovered that unfortunate fact during his engagement to Kate Bennett.

"There's still one more gift." Marco poked at it. "Care to guess what it'll be?"

"Whatever it is, I'll lay odds it has my name on it."

"I think that's pretty much a given."

Stefano ripped open the last package and chuckled softly. His laughter grew in volume as he removed the pair of boxers he found inside, his name stamped across the backside in huge black lettering. "One hundred percent cotton," he informed his brother with a grin. "That's my bride-to-be. A cotton sort of woman."

"I take it you plan to get even?"

"Count on it." He swiveled to face the windows, eyeing Penelope's building. "Though not, I think, with this next one. I promised my bride-to-be a traditional sort of gift and that's precisely what I intend to give her."

He was curious to see how his rational, practical, *logical* Penelope responded.

Stefano's gift to Penelope arrived first thing the next morning.

She took one look inside the box and fell instantly in love—a perfectly rational, practical, *logical* response to what she found there. Or so she'd swear with her dying breath.

CHAPTER SEVEN

STEFANO stormed off the elevator, intent on getting hold
of his soon-to-be fiancée and kissing some sense into
her. Cindy stood up as he approached Penelope's office.
Taking one look at his expression, she ducked down and
hid behind her computer monitor, typing frantically.

He thrust open the office door and slammed it behind
him. To his astonishment, Penelope lay on her couch, a
man in a white lab coat fanning her with a towel. "What
the hell...?"

"Are you a doctor?" the man asked nervously. "I
think she's all right. She just passed out. It happens
sometimes."

"Nellie?" Acute concern overrode his anger and he
started for the couch. "*Cara?* What has happened to
you? Why did you faint?"

Before he could reach the couch, a tiny orange fur
ball leapt into his path, arching its spine and hissing at
him. Penelope jerked upright. "Be careful! Don't step
on Honor."

"Honor?"

"The kitten you sent. That's his name. It's short for
Honorable." She smiled tentatively. "It seemed appropriate, somehow, considering who'd given it to me."

It took an instant for the full implication to sink in.
When it did, Stefano closed his eyes, fighting for control.
Honorable. Did Penelope have any idea what her choice
meant to him? To his astonishment, he found he couldn't
respond to her explanation, the words catching in his

throat. Desperate to give himself a moment to regain his composure, he scooped up the marmalade and crossed to the couch, perching on the arm. Taking his time, he tickled the belly of the animal and was rewarded for his efforts by a loud rumbling purr. The sound held an uncanny resemblance to his bride-to-be's chuckle, Stefano realized, amused.

"Do you like my gift?" he finally managed to ask.

Her face lit up, leaving him in no doubt that she adored the kitten. "You couldn't have picked anything nicer. Thank you."

"My pleasure." The cat curled all four paws around his hand, hooking needle-sharp claws into his flesh. Then, still purring, it gnawed on his finger. Stefano could swear he saw a smug expression gleaming in the animal's amber-colored eyes. He sighed in resignation. Little beast. "Before we discuss the gift you've given me in return, tell me what happened. Why did you faint?"

Her face paled slightly. "It was the pop."

"Pop?"

"When Daniel pierced my ear. I didn't realize it would…" She swallowed. "That it would make such a terrible sound."

She'd caught him by surprise. "*You're* having your ears pierced?"

"Just the one, so we'll match." She frowned. "You didn't think I was going to make you do it unless I was willing to, as well?"

"I assumed your ears were already pierced."

"I never saw the need. Well… Until I decided you should have one done." She lifted a hand to her earlobe, concealing her wince behind a brave smile. "It doesn't hurt too much anymore. How about you?"

"That's why I'm here." Honor gave up ravaging his hand and squirmed for release. He set the kitten down on the couch. It scrambled over Penelope's legs and curled up on her chest. Clearly the cat he'd chosen had excellent taste. He wouldn't mind curling up there, himself. Stefano glanced at Daniel. "Would you excuse us, please? My fiancée and I would like to discuss the situation before proceeding further."

"Of course." The technician addressed Penelope. "Should I call a doctor?"

"That's not necessary." Her gaze turned to Stefano and she smiled happily. "I'll be fine now."

The minute they were alone, he addressed Penelope. "Why did you want me to get my ear pierced?" He fought to keep his tone neutral. "I don't suppose it has anything to do with your effort to tell me from my brother?"

"No!" She jerked upright, tumbling the kitten to her lap. With a horrified gasp, she gathered up the bit of fluff and cuddled it close. Instead of ripping her to shreds it proceeded to lick every inch of bare skin it could reach. "No, that wasn't it at all."

"In that case," he said. "I have a confession to make."

She shifted to make room for him on the couch, drawing her legs beneath her. "Go for it."

"I was very angry when I came here."

Penelope nodded sagely. "Ah. That explains Honor's reaction when you walked in the room. A testosterone to testosterone moment."

Stefano plucked the mewling fur ball from her grasp and studied it with a skeptical expression. "Somehow I doubt that."

Her brows drew together in confusion. "I don't understand. Why were you angry? Because you thought my ear-piercing gift was a clever way to tell you from Marco?''

"Yes.'' He captured her chin in his palm and tilted her head slightly, studying the gold earring she wore. Damn, but it looked painful. "My apologies, *cara*,'' he offered gently. "I see I was mistaken. Instead of being clever and logical about the situation, you were being sweet and romantic.''

"There's no need to be insulting,'' came her indignant protest. "I was not being any such thing. And I resent you suggesting otherwise.''

"Let me guess. That's why you're wearing an earring that's half a heart, right? Because you're being logical?''

Her mouth formed a stubborn line. "Exactly.''

"And I assume if I'd allowed my ear to be pierced, I'd be wearing the other half of the heart?''

A hint of uncertainty crept into her expression. "You don't like it, do you? You think it's a terrible idea.''

"I think it's a brilliant idea,'' he corrected. He set the kitten on the floor and gathered her close. "And as soon as I tell you how much, I'll have Daniel come in and take care of my ear, too.''

Relief caused her eyes to glitter like gold. "Fair warning. Watch out for that pop. It's a killer.''

"I appreciate your concern.''

Her breath trembled between them. "How much do you appreciate it?'' she whispered.

He answered by taking her mouth in a slow, leisurely kiss. She shivered in delight, opening to him with unrestrained passion. The intensity of her response never failed to amaze him. He'd never encountered such sweet generosity in a woman, an openness that ignited a raw intensity within himself, an elemental drive to take and conquer. He knew it wasn't considered politically correct, but when he held her in his arms, all thought deserted him but one—to possess. To brand her with his taste and scent and touch. To make her his own in the most basic way possible.

He deepened the kiss and she drank him in, catching his lower lip and tugging gently. With a soft laugh, he returned the favor, exploring the lush swell of her mouth with his tongue and inhaling her passion-laden moan. She fumbled with the buttons of his shirt, and he couldn't help wondering if she was even aware of her actions. She didn't seem to be the last time.

His buttons came undone beneath her busy hands, then his tie. She tossed the tie over the side of the couch and an ecstatic growl vibrated from the vicinity of the carpet while tiny claws happily ripped into the silk. Hell. The next minute those same claws scaled his leg, digging in with painful determination. No doubt the little beast had come looking for more silk to shred. His error. He'd soon learn his mistress was a cotton type of woman.

"*Cara*—"

"This is nice, isn't it?" she asked with a sigh.

"Delightful. Nellie?"

"Hmm?"

"Your ear guy is waiting outside for us." He peeled her cat off his thigh along with a good portion of skin and handed the bloodthirsty little creature over to Penelope. "As much as I'd like to continue this, I'm afraid we've picked another inconvenient time and place."

She pulled back with notable reluctance, blinking in surprise at his state of undress. "Did I..." She gestured toward his shirt.

"Yes."

"Huh." She cleared her throat. "Imagine that. I'll have to start paying attention to what I'm doing while I'm doing it. I imagine stripping you will be a lot more fun that way."

"I'll make sure of it." He snatched another quick kiss and then released her. Refastening his shirt, he picked up the shredded remains of his tie. Shaking his head in disgust, he shoved it into his pocket and crossed the room to admit Daniel. "We're ready for you now."

The entire procedure only took a brief five minutes. From the way Penelope hovered, he'd have thought it was major surgery. To his private amusement, she covered her ears during the actual piercing. But the minute Daniel left she fluttered around him, admiring the tiny gold half heart that formed the perfect mate to her own.

He grinned at her obvious delight. "Tell me again how this was a practical, rational gift," he said.

"Don't be ridiculous. Of course it was."

"Honey, pierced ears have a certain permanency about them. Or didn't that occur to you?"

"Only if you keep wearing the earring," she pointed out. "The hole will close if you don't."

"Very symbolic."

"You aren't reading more into this than you should, are you?" She snatched up Honor and cuddled him close. "I mean, I could say that giving me a cat smacked of permanency, too."

He frowned. Now that he thought about it, it did. "But our relationship won't be permanent, right?"

"Not at all."

"It's strictly a business proposition."

She avoided his gaze. "Nothing more."

"That's what I thought." He suppressed a smile. "I'll

remind you of that fact after we've been married a year.''

"I won't need a reminder," she insisted.

"Maybe not." He dropped a kiss on the tip of her nose. "But I suspect I will. Have I thanked you for my present, *cara mia?* It was very sweet of you."

"You're welcome. And thank you again for Honor."

"I can't think of a better time and place to express our mutual gratitude." He glanced at the couch, his smile growing. "Can you?"

"I absolutely forbid it."

Penelope blinked at Stefano in astonishment. "Did you actually use the word, 'forbid' in connection with me?"

"You're damned right I did. That cat stays here in my apartment while we go down to the ballroom." He glared at the manipulative kitten who'd quickly learned that by mewling pathetically it could get anything its greedy little heart desired. "One of the advantages to living in the Salvatore penthouse is being able to keep your cat close at hand, wouldn't you agree?"

"Yes, but—"

"One of the disadvantages to living here is that my family always knows where to find me. Which means that as one of the hosts of tonight's function I have precisely—" he checked his watch "—fifteen more minutes to get downstairs before I disgrace my family by being late."

Disgrace? Oh, dear, that would never do. She gave it one final try. "I thought the carrier you bought me for Honor was so I could bring him with us."

"Right. You can bring him from Crabbe and Associates, across the street, to Salvatore's. Which you have now done. It was not meant for you to take him to parties or restaurants or shopping, as you seem inclined to do.'' He stabbed the button for the elevator. ''Stop fussing. Honor will be perfectly comfortable in my apartment now that we've moved the contents of an entire pet store in here.''

She regarded him with acute suspicion. ''Was that a criticism?'' she demanded.

''Not at all, my sweet.'' He ushered her into the car. ''I'm delighted you've decided to buy the beast every cat gadget ever invented.''

''You *are* being sarcastic.'' She planted her hands on her hips. ''I'll have you know that though I adore all your gifts, Honor is special. I've never had a pet before.''

''Which reminds me.'' He hit the emergency button and the elevator ground to a halt. An alarm sounded, which he cut off with a master key. ''Don't you think it's about time you admitted that none of your gifts to me—nor your reaction to the ones I've given you—have been the least bit logical or rational? Confess. They've been emotional choices and emotional reactions to those choices.''

She straightened the frames of the glasses Stefano had given her, a ridiculously delicate and feminine pair of wire rims that weren't in the least practical for a serious-minded business executive. They were also one of half a dozen that had been sent, along with a note that read, ''Just in case we ruin another pair the next time we make love.''

''I'll admit your gifts have been extremely thoughtful,'' she conceded. ''I'll also admit that the only logical response is an excess of gratitude.''

''An excess of gratitude, huh? You mean like this?''

He cupped a hand around her neck and tipped her into his arms. She went willingly, surrendering to the unexpected embrace with an exuberance impossible to disguise. Each time he touched her it became more and more difficult to think straight, and almost as impossible to regain her equilibrium. Not that she tried very hard. She tended to surrender without a murmur of protest, then proceeded to strip him as fast as she could. Not that she was ever aware of—

Her eyes popped open and she pulled back with a gasp. "I did it again, didn't I?"

"Yes." He flicked her hair with his finger. "Though I believe I got even. You look delightfully rumpled."

"This has to stop, Stefano."

To her disgust, he shot her a grin of pure, male satisfaction. "I don't see why. I enjoy rumpling you almost as much as I enjoy getting rumpled."

She turned her back on him and set the elevator in motion once again. Her enthusiasm whenever he touched her worried her. A lot. It warned that her—she winced—*emotions* might actually be engaged. And that would never do. Her relationship with Stefano needed to remain on a business footing. Anything more would be a huge mistake. She tended to make horrific errors in judgment when her emotions were engaged, something she couldn't afford at such a critical juncture.

The elevator slowed and the doors parted, opening to the huge, glittering ballroom on Salvatores' second floor. She risked a quick glance at Stefano. "By the way, I have another present for you." She swept from the car, calling over her shoulder, "Oh, and you might want to check your shirt. You missed a couple of buttons."

She wasn't the only one to notice his shirt, or the trace of lipstick clinging to the corner of his mouth, or the fact that his tie needed to be reknotted. If there'd been any doubt about the extent of their romantic relationship, they'd clarified the situation by their antics in the elevator, a fact brought home to her when she caught a glimpse of herself in a mirror.

As he'd warned, Stefano had left her hair more than a little rumpled and her swollen mouth denuded of lipstick. Barely suppressed passion glittered in her eyes along with a wild, desperate longing. She shook her head in denial, refusing to admit the love-struck woman in the mirror bore any relationship to Penelope Wentworth, business executive.

"So, where's my present?" Stefano asked as soon as he caught up with her.

"It's downstairs in the lobby. Do you want to see it now or later?"

"I think we have a couple of minutes to spare."

A wide, marble staircase led down to the main lobby and they bucked the flow of traffic heading for the gathering. The reaction from those entering the reception was far different than the one at the charity benefit a few weeks ago. Amused grins greeted them, along with a hint of respect.

"I liked the bronze," one man said, grasping Stefano's hand for a quick shake. "Makes quite a powerful statement."

"Bronze?" Stefano murmured in Penelope's ear.

"You'll see."

She led the way to the lobby to where the bronze artwork stood. Stefano slowed as he spotted it, stopping a few feet away. He was silent for so long, she couldn't help wondering if she'd made a terrible error in judgment.

"It's...it's Don Quixote," she offered nervously.

After checking with Luc, she'd had the statue placed right inside the front doors of Salvatores, a silent, noble ambassador greeting all who entered the building.

"So I see."

"I always considered him a symbol of lost causes."

The muscles along Stefano's jaw tightened. "Am I a lost cause? Or is it just that I'm fighting one?"

"Neither." She came up beside him, slipping her hand into his. To her relief, he didn't reject the small gesture. Instead his fingers entwined with hers. "You're fighting against overwhelming odds, knowing it might be impossible to win your battle. But still you'll fight because it's the right thing to do. The honorable decision to make."

"Honor?" he whispered.

"Why do you always act so surprised whenever I say that? It's one of your defining qualities." She leaned into him, sighing in pleasure as he wrapped an arm around her. Did he have any idea how generous and honest he was? Or how rare it was to find a man of his stellar qualities in the business world she inhabited? "I picked up Señor Quixote figuring we could use all the help we could get. What do you think? Shall we ask him to help us tilt at a few windmills?"

"Nellie…"

Her name came out as a soft caress, one that stirred the oddest reaction. A delicious tremor coursed through her, along with a powerful hunger that urged her to slip into his arms again and kiss him until she'd rid them both of every last bit of clothing. Did he have any idea how much she wanted him? How much she—

"You really are determined to ruin your reputation, Ms. Wentworth," Cornell announced from behind, shattering the moment. "Such a shame."

Beside her, Stefano tensed and she slipped an arm around his waist, giving the taut muscles a warning squeeze. "Don't take the bait," she whispered.

"You spoil all my fun," he muttered back.

Penelope spoke before Stefano had the opportunity. "In what way am I ruining my reputation, Mr. Cornell?" she asked.

"By continuing to defend the Salvatores instead of getting out of the way of their imminent self-destruction."

She chuckled in genuine amusement. "I'll take my chances, especially since I suspect the destruction won't be theirs."

"Unlike Salvatore's last fiancée, you're a unique woman." Cornell's gaze shifted to Stefano. "Katie chose to get out of the way, didn't she?"

"With your help," Stefano confirmed.

"I won't deny it, though after being so quick to believe the worst of you, Salvatore, I found I couldn't trust her. Besides, she'd served her purpose by confirming your guilt in the eyes of the world and that's all I cared about." His grin made Penelope nervous. "Unfortunately, disposing of her ended up being...messy."

"Next time, don't dump your women in public."

"One of life's small casualties." Cornell snapped his fingers. "I've been meaning to ask you, Ms. Wentworth. You told me you two were engaged, and yet I don't recall hearing anything official. There isn't a problem, is there? Perhaps you've changed your mind about selling Janus Corp to the Salvatores?"

"We haven't gone public, yet," Penelope said blandly. "Aren't you flattered that you're among the first to know?"

"But I don't see a ring." He made a point of examining her finger. "You're not having second thoughts, are you?"

"Her birthday's not for another week," Stefano interrupted, his words sounding suspiciously like a growl. "She'll get a ring then."

Penelope glared at Cornell. "Thank you so much for ruining the surprise."

He shrugged off her annoyance and turned a mocking gaze on the bronze. "A tarnished statue of an impractical man pursuing lost causes. I can't begin to tell you how appropriate I find this."

It took every ounce of her strength to physically restrain Stefano. "Beating him up isn't going to solve anything," she warned.

"Maybe not, but it'll make me feel a damn sight better. Come on, Cornell." His accent deepened. "Say something else so I can give you what you deserve."

Cornell held up his hands. "No, thanks. And just to prove how generous I am—not to mention forgiving—I've already purchased a wedding gift for you two." Penelope didn't trust his smile one little bit. "I'll make sure you get it the day you tie the knot."

She drew back. "Don't bother. We don't need any presents from you."

"No doubt. But this is one present I insist on delivering whether you want it or not." He bared his teeth. "It'll be my pleasure, though possibly not yours." With that, he headed for the ballroom.

Stefano's hands collapsed into fists. "And you were going to marry that jerk."

Penelope winced. "Don't remind me. Fortunately, good judgment prevailed."

"You mean, fortunately I stepped in and saved your

pretty little backside.'' He slanted her a dry look. ''Purely as a business consideration, of course.''

Her chuckle returned. ''And here I thought it was because you enjoyed how well I stripped you every time we kissed.''

He tucked her close and started for the ballroom. ''That, too, *cara*. That, too.''

She peeked up at him. ''Do you like your statue?''

''No.''

''No!''

''I love my statue,'' he admitted gruffly. Pulling her to a stop, he took her mouth in a swift, passionate kiss. Then he stared down at her with black eyes filled with an emotion she didn't dare name. ''It means more to me than you can know. And one day I'll find a way to repay you.''

''I don't want repayment,'' she protested. ''That's not why I did it.''

Secrets glittered within the darkness of his gaze. ''I know why you did it, probably better than you do. And that, *cara mia,* is how your generosity will be repaid. I'll give you precisely what you've given to me.''

And with those enigmatic words, he escorted her into the ballroom.

Once again, Stefano stormed off the elevator, intent on getting hold of his soon-to-be fiancée and kissing some more sense into her. Not that it had worked last time he tried it. Still, he'd give it his best shot. He hadn't progressed farther than two strides before Loren exited from a nearby office. As much as he'd like to brush past, Stefano knew he couldn't.

''Hello.'' Loren greeted him with the sort of smile people use when they know they should remember the person they were meeting, but couldn't quite place how or why. "Have we met?"

"Stefano Salvatore." Giving in to the inevitable, he held out his hand and braced himself for the customary reaction. To his surprise, it didn't come.

Instead Loren wrinkled his brow in thought. "The name's familiar. I'm afraid I can't quite place it, though."

Stefano's tension eased ever so slightly. "My family owns an extensive import/export business. We're located across the street from you."

"Yes, yes. Of course. You have a reputation for being able to acquire anything anyone might want." Loren smiled knowingly. "For a price, no doubt."

"I've discovered there's always a price to pay whenever we're determined to obtain what we want."

"I can't argue with that. So, tell me, Stefano. What brings you over to our side of the street? Something I can do for you?"

"I'm here to see your niece."

"On business, I assume?"

"Actually it's a social call." Time to put his cards on the table. "Nellie and I have been seeing each other. Perhaps she mentioned?"

"Nellie, huh? Cute nickname. To be honest, Stefano, I'm sure she did tell me about you. I'm equally sure I wasn't giving the matter the attention it deserves." Loren clicked his tongue in dismay. "That's what I get for paying more attention to business than to family. Have you been dating long?"

"A while." Stefano decided to push matters and see what happened. "I guess you'd call it a whirlwind romance."

"A whirlwind romance?" Loren didn't bother to conceal his shock. "With our Penelope?"

Stefano chuckled. "I think it's taken her by surprise, too."

"Well, the best of luck to you. She's a special woman, as I'm sure you're aware."

"Quite special."

"Then I won't delay you further." Loren clapped Stefano on the shoulder. "I assume you know where her office is?"

"Yes, thanks." The query reminded him of why he'd come. He fixed a steely gaze on the office door in question. "If you'll excuse me."

He didn't bother waiting for a response. Brushing past Cindy, he thrust open the door and slammed it closed behind him. It was obvious Penelope had been expecting him. A pleased little smile decorated the mouth he intended to ravish in the next few minutes.

"Give it to me," he demanded.

"I don't know what you're—"

He strode to the window and ripped the drapes apart. The poster was gone. "What did you do with it?"

"I destroyed it."

"The hell you did." He turned and scanned the office. A telltale roll of paper poked out from beneath the cushion of her couch. "Bingo."

"No, wait!" She leapt to her feet and tried to intercept him before he could achieve his goal. "It's mine, Stefano. You can't have it."

"Yes, I can. It's my present and I want it."

"It's *not* your present. The binoculars were your present. This was just—"

He swept her to one side and snagged the rolled-up

poster. "A tease? Your cute way of getting even with me for the lingerie?"

"It was a joke." She tried to take the poster away from him. "Please, Stefano."

"Not until I have a closer look."

Ignoring her protests, he slowly unrolled the paper. Every nerve ending in his body clenched. Nellie—his proper, businesslike, Penelope—had donned the lingerie he'd sent and had a photo taken. She knelt with her back to the camera, smoky nylons caressing every inch of long, slender legs, her pert, rounded bottom showcased by an almost nonexistent pair of panties and garter. Her spine was arched and she'd lifted her hands to the blond waves of hair spilling down her back, the wire-rimmed glasses he'd given her dangling carelessly from her fingertips. And most gut-wrenching of all, she'd turned ever so slightly, exposing the vulnerable curve of her breast.

He fought for breath. "Where the *hell* is the bra I gave you?"

She pointed to the bottom of the poster. Sure enough, the scrap of silk and lace lay discarded at her feet. "I couldn't decide whether I liked this one best or the ones with the bra. The photographer convinced me to go without."

"I'm going to *kill* him."

"Her."

He was only slightly mollified. "Tell me you have every last negative."

"I'm not an idiot. Of course I have all the negatives. I intend to burn them."

"Not a chance."

"I only did it to get back at you for sending that first present."

"You succeeded. You've also caused a riot."

"What are you talking about?"

He carefully rolled the poster. It was either that, or pick up Penelope, dump her on the couch and strip her down to the bits and pieces she'd displayed in the photo. "I'm talking about half the Salvatore employees who were practically falling out of their windows because they were so busy gawking at the poster stuck on your window. One of the more enterprising ones happened to have a pair of binoculars in his office. He was renting them for fifty bucks a minute."

"You're making that up," she scoffed. He gave her a look that had her mouth snapping shut and an attractive shade of pink tinting her cheeks. "You're serious?"

"Dead serious."

"I... He..." She glared. "No one could possibly have known it was me. My arm hides my face."

He glared back. "Everyone knows it's you! You sent the damned binoculars."

"So, I sent you binoculars." She shrugged. "What difference does that make?"

"They arrived in the middle of a family meeting. I have five brothers. It didn't take them long to figure out what they should do with your gift."

Her complacency vanished. "How could you?" she stormed. "The binoculars were for *you*, not your brothers."

"Let me repeat. I have *five* brothers. The odds were not in my favor." He smiled grimly. "Although you won't have any trouble telling me from Marco for the next few days. He'll be the one sporting the black eye."

"You didn't!"

"I sure did." He held out his hand. "The negatives."

"You can't have them."

"Consider them a wedding present."

"We're not getting married, yet. We're not even engaged."

"Wrong. After that cute stunt, we're going to announce our engagement immediately and follow it with a ceremony on your birthday. It's the only way to protect you."

She stared in utter bewilderment. "Protect me?"

"That's right. Because the first wisecrack said in my presence is going to be met with a fist. I suspect a ring on your finger will keep most comments in check."

"You'd hit someone just because they said something snide about me?"

He struggled to control the fury surging through him, fought to keep his voice low and nonthreatening. Judging by the alarm flickering in her gold eyes, he'd failed miserably. "You don't know what it is to lose your reputation. You don't know what it is to have people whisper behind your back, to look at you as though you'd crawled out of a cesspool. I do. If there's any way I can prevent your going through that, I will."

Compassion darkened her gaze. "Oh, Stefano."

"I don't want pity!"

"It's just a risqué poster," she whispered. "It won't affect my reputation."

"Don't you understand? By marrying me, you'll be tarred with my brush. Crabbe and Associates' standing in the community will keep most of the talk in check. But not all of it. Not if Cornell decides to cause trouble. When our relationship ends, it will be with your reputation intact. I refuse to allow our marriage to cause you any trouble. I'll do everything in my power to protect you from that."

"Do you really think the poster will damage my reputation? Don't you think that's a bit Victorian?"

"I'm not taking any chances. Once we're married, it won't be an issue. With luck, the blame will fall on me. They'll think I've been a bad influence." He offered a crooked smile. "And they'll be right. Somehow I doubt you'd have pulled this crazy stunt with anyone else."

A knock sounded at the door and Loren glanced in. "Am I interrupting?"

"Not at all," Penelope greeted him with unmistakable warmth. "Come on in and let me make introductions."

Loren crossed the room and offered his hand to Stefano. "Hello, there," he said with a friendly smile. "Have we met?"

CHAPTER EIGHT

STEFANO recovered swiftly, smoothing over the briefest of awkward pauses by returning Loren's handshake. "Stefano Salvatore. Good to see you."

"The name's familiar." Loren wrinkled his brow. "But I can't quite place where I've heard it before."

Stefano slanted a quick glance toward Penelope, not in the least surprised to see the tightness edging her mouth. "My family runs an import/export business. Our building is directly across from yours."

"You're a friend of Penelope's?"

"We're good friends."

"Business?" Loren probed delicately.

"Personal."

"Penelope," her uncle chided. "Shame on you for being so secretive."

"It's all very sudden, Uncle Loren," she hastened to explain. "Perhaps we could have dinner together later this week so you and Stefano have an opportunity to get better acquainted."

"Excellent idea." As though suddenly recalling why he'd come, he held out a folder. "Cindy said you were looking for this. I don't know how it ended up on my desk. I guess someone dropped it off by mistake."

Stefano could feel the tension pouring off Penelope and experienced a twinge of sympathy. She'd been carrying an impossible burden for some time now. Fortunately for her, it was one he'd soon share. "Thank you for finding it for me," she murmured.

"My pleasure." Loren held out his hand again. "Good to meet you, Stefano. I look forward to that dinner."

The minute the older man left, Stefano turned and faced Penelope. "Something you'd care to tell me, *cara?*"

"No."

"You're certain?"

She had trouble meeting his gaze. No surprise there. "Positive."

"Perhaps I should mention that your uncle and I met out in the hallway right before I walked in here." He allowed her a moment to assimilate that bit of information before continuing. "He didn't recognize me just now. I can only think of one explanation to account for that."

She lifted her chin, refusing to back down. It was a brazen approach, he'd give her that. Too bad it wouldn't work. "Really?" she said in a surprisingly composed voice. "And what would that explanation be?"

"Your uncle is the small matter that would compromise the interests of Crabbe and Associates, the one you couldn't tell me about. What's wrong with him? Alzheimer's? Dementia? Early senility?"

"Please, Stefano—"

"You're protecting both your uncle and the firm by getting married and taking control away from him. And you're hoping to do it before word leaks about his condition. Am I right so far?"

"You know I can't answer that," she retorted.

An irrational fury gripped him. "Because you're afraid if you tell me the truth I'll pass on the information?" His Italian accent grated, even on his own ears, betraying the depths of his pain. "After all, I'm Stefano Salvatore."

"*Stop it!*" She turned on him and he realized he'd pushed her to the breaking point. "I have a responsibility to my companies. I couldn't tell you about Loren. I couldn't tell *anyone*. Have you any idea what would happen if word got out?"

He knew precisely what would happen. "The value of your company would take a nosedive. You'd also start losing contracts."

"Exactly. I don't care for myself. But what would happen to my employees, to all the individuals dependent on my company? I have to put their best interests ahead of my own. It isn't a matter of not trusting you, Stefano."

"And now that I've uncovered your secret?"

She waved that aside as if it were of no account. "Credit me with some intelligence. You won't say anything."

"You're so positive?"

"You want to know how positive I am? You won't even tell your family. And from what I've seen, you Salvatores tell each other everything." She poked her finger against his chest. "I'll go you one better. Even if you were to tell them, the information would stop right there."

Her certainty pleased him, perhaps because she hadn't based it in logic, but rather on sheer instinctive emotion. But most important of all... She trusted him. "That said, you'd rather they not find out."

She inclined her head. "The more people aware of the problem, the greater the risk that something inadvertent will be said. I've had a difficult enough time covering for him."

He didn't doubt that for a minute. "So now we marry and you gain your inheritance by assuming control of Crabbe. What then?"

"When I first approached you with my proposition, you thought I wanted to make a power grab. I didn't. I don't want to take over the business." She twisted her hands together. "I want to get rid of it."

He couldn't conceal his shock. "Nellie—"

"It's decided, Stefano," she said, her tone adamant. "I'm going to sell Crabbe and Associates. I'm well aware of my own limitations. I'm not qualified to step into my uncle's shoes. That's all there is to it."

"What will you do instead?"

"I suspect there will be plenty of job offers to assess. I enjoy the corporate world. I'm good at what I do and I intend to continue working." She shrugged. "Just not as head of a company the size of Crabbe. I prefer something smaller and more intimate. Fortunately the profits from the sale will give me time to make up my mind, though I'm giving the bulk of the money to Loren. Considering he and my father were the ones who made the firm into what it is, he's more than earned it."

"If that's what you want to do, I'll support your decision. I will say, it's a shame to have the business pass out of your family after all your father and uncle have done to build it." He gathered her close, sliding a thumb across the arch of her cheekbone. "How long have you been dealing with this?"

She released her breath in a tired sigh. "I started noticing small slips about a year ago, but kept dismissing each new incident. Then he blew a huge account and I couldn't ignore the situation any longer. I suggested last month that we sell Crabbe and Associates."

"I assume Loren refused?"

"He wouldn't hear of it. I think he's afraid. Agreeing to sell means acknowledging his disease and he can't bring himself to do that." She relaxed against Stefano, a regretful smile playing about her mouth. "I guess the need to be in control runs in the family."

"How will he react when you take over?"

"He won't have any choice. He'll bluster. But secretly I suspect he'll be relieved."

Stefano took a moment to consider their options. Not that there were many. In fact, he could only come up with one. "You realize our marriage has become imperative now. If word gets out about Loren, you'll never be able to sell the business for what it's worth."

"I'm well aware of that."

He reached into his pocket and removed a small jeweler's box. "I've been carrying this around with me for the past few days, waiting for the right moment. I think that moment's arrived." He flipped open the lid and removed the ring, a ruby and diamond entwined in the shape of a heart. Taking her hand in his, he slid the ring onto her finger. "Will you marry me, Nellie?"

"It's beautiful," she whispered unsteadily. "Rubies are my birthstone."

"And diamonds are mine. That's why I chose this particular ring." His voice deepened. "The jeweler told me that rubies mean devotion and integrity, and that diamonds represent invincibility and good fortune. I can only hope he's right."

She smiled through her tears. "They also represent innocence, something I'm hoping we'll soon prove."

"It's a good combination, Nellie. A winning combination." He pulled her close again. "What do you say? Will you marry me?"

"You know I will."

"You won't regret it. I'll help you take care of this. I'll make sure you're protected." He lowered his mouth to hers. "I promise."

"Nervous?" Stefano asked.

Penelope glanced at the door leading to the judge's chambers and nodded. "A little," she admitted. "It helps that we decided to get married in San Francisco. I don't think I could have handled a trip to Vegas."

"I prefer marrying at home, too. That way we can return to my apartment for our wedding night."

Oh, dear heaven. Their wedding night. She straightened her beaded ivory suit jacket with trembling hands. "Good idea. We'll also be able to have Honor with us."

"Right. The cat," he muttered. "Just what I wanted on my honeymoon."

"It's not a honeymoon! It's a—"

"A wedding night. Close enough." She lapsed into silence at that and he eyed her with uncomfortable intensity. "I brought something I hoped would make you less nervous. But I have the nasty feeling it'll only make matters worse."

"What is it?"

"Here." He offered a beautifully wrapped box.

"Please let this be something sweet and silly." That way it would match what she'd gotten him.

"'Fraid not." His mouth curved into a wry smile. "I'm guessing it's going to be one of those emotional moments you despise so much."

"I appreciate the warning." She opened the box and closed her eyes, fighting to draw breath. "Oh, Stefano. What have you done?"

He gently removed a short lace veil, clearly decades old. "My great-grandmother came from Burano and made this for my mother's wedding day. None of the other Salvatore brides have had an opportunity to wear it, since their weddings have all been a trifle...unconventional. You'll be the first."

She fought to keep her tone light. "Ours is considered conventional?"

Stefano shrugged. "Believe it or not, it is compared to the rest of my brothers."

"Frightening."

"I think the veil qualifies as something old, as well as something borrowed."

"Why are you doing this?" Her mouth trembled and she pressed her lips together before continuing. "It's not like we'll have a real marriage."

"You're wrong," he corrected. "This will be a real marriage. You just haven't figured that out, yet." He carefully positioned the veil on Penelope's head and tucked a lock of hair behind her ear. "And I'm doing it because you don't have anyone else to take care of these sorts of details. If your mother were alive—or mine, for that matter—she'd have made sure you had something old and something new."

"Something borrowed and something blue?" she finished the rhyme in a husky voice.

"Coming right up." He reached into the box and removed two gold and lapis lazuli butterfly clips to hold the veil in place. "And these, *cara,* take care of new and blue. I picked them up before coming here."

Tears gathered on the tips of her lashes as he fastened the clips. "Now I'm too embarrassed to give you my gift."

He smiled at her, his gaze full of a delicious tenderness. "Come, sweetheart. Show me what you bought."

Reluctantly she handed over the small round canister.

"I hope your sense of humor is intact. Otherwise I'm in serious trouble."

It only took a moment for him to shred the paper. His shout of laughter went a long way toward easing her tension. "Tarnish remover?"

A hesitant smile quivered at the corners of her mouth. "Think it'll work?"

"If you're the one applying it, I'm positive it will."

"Mr. Salvatore? Ms. Wentworth?" the clerk interrupted. "The judge will see you now."

"Ready?" Penelope asked.

Stefano took her hand in his. "I've been ready almost from the start."

She wished she had the chance to question him about what he meant, but there wasn't an opportunity before they were ushered into the judge's chambers. Aside from exchanging a few pleasantries, the judge got right to the business at hand. The entire procedure was shockingly brief, though Penelope found the vows they spoke more powerful and moving than she'd anticipated. By the time they were pronounced man and wife, she was in tears again.

Stefano brushed the telltale moisture from her cheeks. "Don't cry, *cara*. Be happy."

"I am," she managed to say through her tears. "I'm very happy."

Gathering her close he kissed her as though he really were a bridegroom in love with his bride, rather than a business partner entering a temporary contract. And then he said something that truly panicked her. Smiling down at her with a passion she couldn't mistake, he whispered, "You're mine now, Mrs. Salvatore."

"Well, it's done."

The words didn't sound quite as casual as Penelope

had hoped. Instead there was a self-conscious hesitancy to them. Perhaps it had something to do with the way Stefano had said, *"You're mine now, Mrs. Salvatore"* the minute the wedding vows had been spoken. Or perhaps it was because this was her wedding night and the idea of spending it with Stefano filled her with an odd combination of urgency and anxiety.

Picking up Honor, he put the kitten in the hallway before firmly closing the door on its disgruntled meow. "Yes, it's done."

She removed the veil her husband had given her a few short hours ago and placed it gently on his dresser, along with the butterfly clips that had held it in place. It still came as a distinct shock to realize she had a husband. She peeked at him from beneath her lashes, aware that he'd been watching her every move with unwavering concentration.

"Now that we're married, I guess that means I'm in charge," she thought to mention.

He lifted an eyebrow at that. "Excuse me?"

She faced him. "When we were at Benjamin's hammering out the conditions of our marriage, you agreed that I'd be in charge of all marital decisions."

"Did I?" He shrugged off his tux jacket and draped it over a chair. "That was rather foolish of me."

"I wouldn't call it foolish. I think it was a sound business decision on your part."

"No doubt." He stretched, his dress shirt pulled taut across a broad chest and impressive shoulders. She hastened to look away. "No doubt you also think I made it based on careful analysis and rational deduction."

"No," she corrected with a gruff chuckle. "That's

how I make decisions. You tend to allow emotion to interfere with your decision-making process.''

He greeted the assessment with a bland smile. "Do I?''

"Yes, you do.'' The expression in his eyes unnerved her. But she didn't dare back down. It would give him the upper hand. And after only a few short hours of marriage, that would never do. "For instance, your wedding gifts were an emotional decision. Romantic, but emotional.''

"Did you like them?''

She couldn't lie. Not about that. "Very much.''

"I wanted our marriage to be memorable.''

"You mean our business arrangement.''

He closed the distance between them. "No, *cara*.'' He slid his arms around her and pulled her close. "I mean our marriage.'' He lowered his head and brushed a kiss along her jawline.

"What are you doing?'' she asked, shivering beneath the delicate caress.

"I'm kissing my wife.''

"I...I didn't tell you to do that.''

"True. You also didn't tell me not to. I assume you're pleased at my show of initiative?'' he prodded.

She could feel herself giving in and fought it. "I don't think this is a good idea.''

"I think it's an excellent one.''

"You're planning on consummating our relationship, aren't you?''

"The thought had occurred to me.''

"And if I don't want to?''

He lifted his head. "Are you ordering me to stop?''

Something in his voice warned her to tread very, very carefully. "I'd rather not make it an order.''

"Good decision."

"But I will try to talk you out of it. You must see that this isn't terribly practical. There's no reason—no sound business reason, that is—for us to sleep with each other."

"Then we won't sleep. We'll just make love."

Before she could formulate any further arguments, he urged her backward toward the bed. She sank onto the mattress and Stefano knelt on the floor in front of her. Cupping her face, he feathered another kiss across her mouth.

"Trust me, Nellie."

"You know I do."

"Then admit that what's between us has nothing to do with business. For once in your life admit that there's a time and place for a sheer emotional response to a situation, and we've discovered that perfect time and place."

She shook her head, fighting the truth. "This isn't what I intended to have happen. I planned to marry so I could protect my business. I wasn't supposed to feel..." She looked at him, fighting tears. "I wasn't supposed to want you."

"Then why choose me?" he demanded urgently. "Why didn't you marry someone off the streets? Someone who'd sign a prenup and leave quietly after you'd gained control of Crabbe and Associates?"

"Because I didn't trust just anyone. I trusted you."

His brows drew together. "You were so certain of me?"

Did he doubt it? It was her turn to cup his face, to trace the hard, masculine sweep of jaw and cheekbone with fingers that showed a distressing tendency to tremble. "I thought so after I read my investigator's report and realized how badly everyone had misjudged you. Once I met you, I knew. How anyone could suspect you'd commit an unethical act is beyond comprehension.''

''You're that sure?'' His control slipped for an instant, allowing her a glimpse of the torment beneath his stoic exterior.

''I'm that sure,'' she confirmed with utter sincerity.

He thanked her with a long, lingering kiss. ''And I'm sure that I've never met a woman I want more than you.''

She caught the shift in his mood, the gathering tension along his chest and shoulders and the burn of hunger in his gaze. Her breath grew shallow as she waited for him to make the next move. And then waiting seemed an impossible task. She knew what she wanted, as clearly as Stefano had known. He might prefer to wrap it up in pretty emotions, but she could be practical. She needed a physical outlet for the passions straining for release. It didn't mean she'd lost control. It simply meant that she'd chosen the best of several options, the one that would offer them both the most benefit.

Taking a deep breath, she said, ''If I kiss you, I can get you out of those clothes in no time.''

Joy exploded in his gaze, threatening her precious control. ''Then I suggest you kiss me.''

She didn't require any further prompting. Wrapping her arms around him, she availed herself of the most delicious mouth she'd ever sampled, plundering the depths with insatiable, biting kisses. He matched her, the give-and-take between them rapidly escalating out of control. When she opened her eyes again, she'd managed to bare Stefano to the waist. To her astonishment, her suit jacket had also disappeared, leaving only a scrap

of silk and lace behind—one of the pieces of lingerie
Stefano had sent a few short weeks earlier.

"You're so beautiful," he murmured.

She doubted that. She couldn't possibly be as beautiful as Stefano. His bronzed skin traced its origins to
warm, flavorful Mediterranean climes, the taut expanse
layered over corded sinew and banded muscle. She ran
her fingers across his shoulders and down well-devel-
oped biceps, feeling the ripple of power beneath her
hands. He was strong of form and character, sweeping
aside all restraint with a simple touch. A smile of acknowledgment teased her mouth. At least, he swept aside
her restraint.

He sketched the lacy edge of her bra, and her nipples
tightened, betraying the intensity of her desire. "Tell me
what you want," he urged.

"Take it off me."

Her bra fell away and he captured the weight of her
breasts in his palms, circling the tips with repeated
sweeps of his thumbs, catching each of her helpless
moans with a drugging kiss. "More?" he asked.

"Oh, yes. Much, much more."

Her skirt disappeared next, slipping off her hips with
a bit of masculine assistance, and she fell backward onto
the bed, splayed across the black comforter. It had to be
the most decadent feeling she'd ever experienced. As
much as she'd like to blame it on the silk beneath her,
she knew it was due to the man standing in front of her.
Just looking at him filled her with a desperate want.

He stripped off his clothing and joined her on the
mattress, kissing a path from her stocking-covered calves
to the spot on her thighs where the nylons ended. Her
reaction hit hard. A bone-deep shuddering tensed every
muscle while a burning heat coalesced in loins damp

with desire. Ever so gently he cupped her and she arced in reaction, her hands fisting in the comforter. She strained to speak, to move, to plead for a possession she'd wasted so much time denying.

She managed to push out a single word. "Please."

"I will," he promised. It only took a moment to strip away the last of her clothing. "I want you, you know that, don't you?"

A chuckle escaped, low and deep and darkly intimate. "A very logical reaction given the circumstances."

"I thought so."

The laughter died away, replaced by a painful yearning. "Kiss me, Stefano."

"As a business associate or as your husband?"

She reached for him, pulling him into her arms. "As my husband. As the man I trust with all my secrets."

He responded instantly to her comment. He took her mouth in a kiss that drove every thought from her head, staking a claim she couldn't refute. His hands seemed to be everywhere at once, sweeping a path of fire across her breasts and down her belly. Tracing tantalizing circles from the inside of her thighs upward to the moist core of her. Delving into her warmth until it grew to an inferno. Coaxing. Driving. Tempting her until she was incoherent with need.

"What do you want?" he whispered the insidious words.

"More. I want more."

"Why?"

"Because."

"Tell me, *cara.*"

She shook her head in confusion. Why didn't he take her? Why didn't he give them what they both needed?

"Please, Stefano. I don't understand what you're asking."

"Yes, you do. I'm asking you to give all of yourself to me."

"You have it! You know you do."

"No, sweetheart. You're holding back." He gathered her close. "I know you're afraid. Don't be."

"I still don't understand. What do you want from me?" The words were torn from her, desperate and pleading. "Just tell me and it's yours."

"I want your surrender. You said you trust me. If you do, then don't hold anything back. Surrender yourself. I'll protect you. I swear I will."

She couldn't answer. Not with words. Instead she rose to meet him, arching upward and opening herself to him. He surged into her warmth, joining them indelibly with one deep thrust. She'd never felt anything so incredible or so natural. They locked together, forming a whole, mated into one.

"Give yourself to me, my love," he urged once more. "All of yourself."

Even as she abandoned physically to him, she fought his demand, desperate to keep some small part safely shut away. He cupped her buttocks, lifting her, filling her, taking her again and again. From deep inside, from a closely protected place, an unfurling began, a glorious blossoming. It leaked out, then poured out, streaming forth in hungry waves. The tidal force surged through her, sweeping past every defense and all barriers, ripping her apart until she had no choice but to do as he'd asked and surrender that darkest place.

"Stefano!" It was a cry of ultimate capitulation and they both knew it.

He drove into her a final time, melding them, fusing

their bodies and hearts and souls. Understanding hit hard, an alarming awareness that she'd been changed in some fundamental, irrevocable way. She battled the inevitable with ever fiber of her being, but it was impossible to win this particular war. And as that knowledge branded her, she lost control. Utterly. The Penelope that had been no longer existed. In her place Nellie rose, eclipsing what had come before. It was Stefano—her husband—who had wrought the change. And in that moment of deepest passion she called to him, whispered to him words that bound them together.

She gave to him the sweetest of promises—her unconditional surrender.

CHAPTER NINE

WHEN Penelope awoke, morning light had just begun to creep into Stefano's bedroom. *Their* bedroom, she hastened to correct herself. They were married now, committed for an indefinite period by the words they'd spoken and the physical bond they'd forged during the night. Slipping from beneath the covers, she searched through the suitcase she'd brought with her the day before. It contained a small selection of clothing that would suffice until she could make arrangements to have the rest of her possessions moved to the penthouse suite.

At the very bottom of her case, she found a short cotton nightgown trimmed in eyelet lace—a compromise she'd found amusing when she'd purchased the garment, since it offered the cotton she preferred along with the lace Stefano found so appealing. Slipping it over her head, she gathered up her glasses, a notepad, and a pen, and returned to bed. Honor slipped into the room and clawed his way onto the mattress, curling up in her lap. She stroked his cream-and-yellow striped fur, soothed by the buzzing rumble vibrating through the kitten.

Flipping open the notepad, she frowned at the blank page as she collected her thoughts. She wanted to jot down a few notes before Stefano awoke. Just one or two reminders of how she hoped their marriage would proceed, because one thing she knew for certain—it couldn't continue as it had started. That decided, she began her list, becoming swiftly engrossed.

"Item number three's acceptable, but I flat-out refuse to have anything to do with number one."

She started at the sound of Stefano's sleep-roughened voice, her pen gouging a hole in her paper. Honor squawked an indignant protest before hopping off the bed in search of a more comfortable—and less jumpy—place to nap.

"I didn't realize you were awake," Penelope said, shooting him an uneasy glance.

"Obviously. Otherwise you wouldn't have put this on." He hooked his finger around the strap of her nightgown and tugged. "Not when you knew I'd have to go to all the trouble of removing it again."

"Don't bother."

"Oh, it's no bother." His eyes looked downright wicked, a trick of the dawn light, no doubt. How unnerving. "I can't help but notice that it's cotton."

"I like cotton."

"You didn't yesterday."

She capped her pen and flipped her notebook closed. "Yesterday was an aberration."

"I'd rather you not refer to our wedding day as an aberration." Folding his arms behind his head, he yawned, looking entirely too large and male and invasive. "So why do you want to change the direction of our marriage?"

She shoved her glasses on top of head. Considering Stefano's tone of voice, she preferred having him a bit out of focus. It seemed safer somehow. "I don't think this is the appropriate time to discuss—"

He rapped a finger against her notebook. "Number one on your list. You want to change directions. Why?" he demanded. "Is it because you lost control last night and allowed your emotions to get the better of you? Is that why you want to change things?"

His darling wife blinked back at him with impressive innocence, her eyes vaguely unfocused. "Excuse me? I have no idea what you're talking about."

Muttering an Italian imprecation, he plucked her glasses from the top of her head and propped them on the tip of her nose. "Can you hear me now?"

Her chin jutted out at a defiant angle. "I could hear you before."

"Funny. I thought your loss of sight had also affected your hearing." He eyed her keenly. "Don't you think it's about time you tell me why you're so obsessed with separating emotions from your business dealings?"

"It's sensible," she answered promptly.

He shot her a warning look. "I'm not an idiot. I can tell there's a reason for all this sensible behavior. Come, *cara*. Confess. What deep, dark secret are you keeping from me?"

He wasn't surprised when she glanced away. Stubborn to the end. "It's a reasonable decision based on—"

"Enough!"

She escaped the bed, scattering her notebook and pen as she fled. Halfway across the room, she swung around to confront him, her nightgown belling around the slender thighs he'd taken such pleasure kissing the night before. "You want to know? Fine. I'll tell you. I no longer allow my emotions to influence my decisions because I made that mistake years ago."

"And paid for it?"

She shook her head, the tousled waves of her hair tumbling to her shoulders in enticing disarray. "Oh, no. I wasn't the one stuck paying."

The strap of her nightgown drifted down her arm

again, revealing the upper curve of one lush breast. Between the tormented expression on her face, her rumpled golden hair and short, not-so innocent white nightie, she looked like a fallen angel facing execution. He fought off the temptation to sweep her into his arms and return her to their bed. Later, he promised himself. First they'd finish their discussion. This moment was long overdue and he refused to do anything to jeopardize its occurrence.

"I'm forced to disagree, love," he deliberately provoked. "I suspect you paid dearly for whatever happened."

She exploded, just as he'd hoped. For such an unemotional woman, she certainly had a surfeit of emotions, an irony that seemed to have escaped her notice. If it weren't so serious, it would be amusing. "I wasn't the one who paid the price," she announced, wrapping her arms around her waist. "The employees of Janus Corp took care of that for me. They were the ones who paid dearly."

"How?"

Her mouth quivered, despite her attempts to suppress the telltale tremor. "You should have seen me at twenty-one, Stefano. I was quite the corporate woman, despite my age. Ambitious. Hard-nosed. Disgustingly sure of myself and my abilities. After all, I'd been living and breathing the heady corporate air since age ten. I was certain I knew it all."

"You probably knew a good deal more than most people your age," he soothed.

"But not enough!" She paced the floor. "I was arrogant. I demanded control of my own company so I could prove my brilliance to the world at large. I talked

Loren into giving me Janus to run as I saw fit. He didn't want to do it. We had the most horrendous battles.''

"I gather you won in the end?"

"Oh, he gave me control, all right. But I'm not sure you could call it winning.''

"Something went wrong."

"Something went very wrong." Her hands closed into fists. "Janus was a small import/export firm, nowhere near as big as Salvatores or Cornell's firm. But it had potential. A month after I waltzed through the front doors I discovered that someone was using Janus as their private black market outlet. Pirated copies of major motion picture releases were being funneled out of the country through Janus. So were computer software programs. And chips and video games. It was an impressive list.''

Stefano stared, stunned. "What the hell did you do?"

"I—" She hesitated. "First, tell me what you would have done."

He answered promptly. "I'd have found who was responsible and turned him over to the authorities, along with whatever proof I'd obtained."

"An excellent solution. But not the one I chose." She stalked to the windows and swept aside the drapes. Brilliant sunshine poured over her, bleaching the color from her face and throwing her profile into stark relief. "I was furious. Someone had used my company—used *me*—for illegal profit. The minute I found out about it, I fired them.''

"The guilty parties?"

"Not even close. I fired all the top echelon people. Every last one of them." Her laugh was painful to hear. "I denounced them publicly, said they were responsible, regardless of the actual culprit because they were the ones in charge and therefore the fault was theirs.''

Stefano threw back the covers and joined her at the window, wrapping his arms around her. "Did you ever find the person behind it all?"

"It was—" Her voice broke and she bowed her head. "It was a shipping clerk. Oh, Stefano. A lowly shipping clerk. And I'd destroyed the reputation of all those key personnel because I'd made an impulsive decision. I'd reacted in the heat of anger, instead of assessing the situation calmly and rationally. If I'd waited..." She stumbled to a halt.

"What did Loren do?"

"Nothing," she whispered. "I begged him to fix things, but he wouldn't. He said I'd wanted the responsibility and now I'd have to learn how to handle the consequences that came with it."

Stefano massaged the taut muscles knotting her shoulders. "I know you, Nellie. You would have done everything in your power to correct the situation."

"I made a public apology and helped most of my former employees find new positions. But it wasn't enough. It will never make up for what I'd done to them."

"*Cara—*"

She turned in his arms. "Now do you understand why I sympathize with what you're going through? Why I'm so certain you're innocent? Right from the start I looked at your situation logically. I researched. I made a thorough analysis. I didn't leap to conclusions. I didn't base my decision on emotion or instinct. And I never will."

"You have got to be kidding. Every last decision you've made has been based on emotion and instinct. At least the ones in regard to me."

She stared at him with a bewilderment that tore at his heart. "Don't be ridiculous. I've been totally logical about the Bennett situation."

"No, you haven't," he argued. "You've dismissed all the facts against me without any proof to the contrary."

"You're wrong! How can you say that?"

"I can say it because it's true." He fought for patience. "You've stood up for me from the start without a shred of evidence supporting my innocence. Don't get me wrong. I appreciate your faith—"

"You're welcome!"

"There's no need for sarcasm, love. The only reason I'm bothering to bring this up is that damned list of yours." He inclined his head toward the notebook she'd dumped on the floor. "You intend to change the conditions of our marriage and I'm not about to let that happen."

"I'm not trying to change them, just return to our original agreement. Last night—"

"Last night scared the hell out of you." She wouldn't like this next part, but it had to be said. "That's why you want to change things. Because you're terrified."

She shoved against his chest, struggling to free herself from his hold. "Have you lost your mind? That's not it at all."

"Yes, it is." He tightened his grasp, refusing to release her. "You lost control last night. And this morning, after having entirely too much time to reflect, you've suddenly discovered that your emotions are engaged and you're panicking. You didn't expect to feel anything for me, and that's why you're so afraid. You're afraid because it's too late. No matter what you say or how hard you fight, there *is* an emotional connection between us. The choices and decisions you've made in our relationship haven't been the least logical. And now you're doing everything in your power to hide from the truth. To deny what is.''

"No!"

"Dammit, Nellie. You didn't just marry me to save your business." How could she ignore the truth, especially after what they'd shared? "If that's all you wanted, you could have chosen some safe, easily manipulated Joe off the streets. But you didn't. You chose me, even though you knew we'd never be able to maintain an emotional distance."

"We can." She glared at him. "At least, *I* can."

"Be honest, Nellie. You've sensed the connection between us from the start. Hell, we both go up in flames every time we touch. You're trembling even now. And with each day that passes, with each kiss and caress we exchange, with each new occasion we make love, we tighten the bonds between us. The *emotional* bonds."

She fought the suggestion for all she was worth. "It's lust. A...a physical release. Chemistry."

"It's love."

He'd said the forbidden and she wriggled free of his grasp in a flat-out panic. "No! No, don't use that word."

"Why?" He captured her again, thrusting his hands into her hair and tipping her head back until their gazes clashed. "Because you're afraid of it? Because the parents you loved died, taking that love with them? Because the uncle you adored, though kind and hardworking, didn't understand what it was to love a child? Because you were taught, in the most ruthless way possible, that strong emotions will destroy you?"

"Stop it!" She covered her ears. "I can't think straight."

He pried her hands free. "What about the gifts you

gave me? They were gifts from the heart, Nellie. Gifts that delivered little pieces of yourself into my keeping. They're treasures that I'll protect and hold safe for the rest of my life.''

She was crying, great heaving sobs. ''I can't love you. If I do—''

''*What?* What terrible thing will happen, *cara?*''

''I'll make a mistake!'' Her expression pleaded with him, begged for his understanding. ''I'll make another horrific mistake. Like I did with Janus.''

''Or maybe you'll just make decisions with your heart instead of your head. Not with anger. Not with rational deductive analysis. But with love and compassion and the sort of generosity that's such a natural part of your personality.''

She hit him with her only weapon—words. ''You're wrong. You're romanticizing our relationship. I slept with you, Stefano. But it wasn't out of love. It was lust, pure and simple.''

''There's nothing pure or simple about lust,'' he informed her gently. ''Don't throw away something that's so vital to us both.''

She drew away, freezing him with an icy, golden stare. ''I don't love you, Stefano. I'm sorry if you read something more into our relationship than there was.''

He simply smiled. ''I didn't, Nellie.'' He headed for the bathroom, pausing at the door to glance back at her. ''Fair warning, *cara*. When you taint something beautiful, you'll find it takes more than tarnish remover to repair the damage. Don't tarnish what's between us. You may never get it to shine again.''

An hour later, Penelope entered the empty elevator at Salvatores and punched the button that would take her to Stefano's office. All she could think about was getting to her husband as quickly as possible. She fought a rush of tears, brushing her fingertips impatiently across the tips of her lashes. Tears were so irrational. She hated when she gave in to them. They served no purpose whatsoever, other than as a pure feminine release. Far better to deal with the situation, than to succumb to an emotional outburst.

The instant the doors parted, she hastened from the car. A knot of Salvatores stood at the far end of the hall and she wondered if they'd already heard what had happened. She could only hope that they hadn't and she could get to Stefano before the news broke. She raced down the corridor, brushing by what seemed an endless number of brothers-in-law. Ignoring their questions, she finally spotted Stefano. Thrusting Marco from her path, she threw herself into her husband's arms and promptly gave into a pure feminine release to end all pure feminine releases.

She burst into noisy tears.

"What's happening?" she heard Pietro ask.

"Stefano made Penelope cry."

"What the hell did you do to her?" Luc demanded.

"Maybe she didn't want Stefano at all. Maybe she meant to cry on Marco's shoulder."

Marco merely grinned. "I do believe our dear sister-in-law has finally learned to tell which of us is her husband."

Stefano wrapped his wife in a protective embrace. "*Cretinos!* Can't you see something has happened? Give her some space." He tipped her face up to his. "What's wrong, Nellie? Why are you crying?"

"Oh, Stefano. The most awful thing has happened.

The news just broke.'' She drew a shuddering breath. ''You're being tarnished again.''

''Calm down, sweetheart. Try to be logical, for once.''

''How many times do I have to explain?'' Anger swept away her tears. ''I'm always logical.''

''Of course,'' he soothed. ''Now tell me how I'm being tarnished.''

She fought for composure with only limited success. ''The reporter said you'd given them the information.''

''What information?''

''About Loren. Someone leaked the facts about his medical condition. And everyone is saying it's you.''

Stefano looked at his brothers. ''Pietro, check it out. Discover what's going on. Luc, I could use your help on this. See if you can find who really broke the story.''

''I think we can guess.''

''I don't want guesswork. I want proof.''

''That might not be possible.''

''Make it possible!'' With that, Stefano gathered Penelope close and strode down the hall toward his office. Once inside, he settled her onto the couch. Crossing to the small wet bar, he poured a brandy. ''Come, *cara*. Drink this and tell me what you know.''

Penelope took the snifter and managed a small sip. ''A reporter for *Financial News* called to confirm facts he had regarding Loren's health.''

''I assume you denied it.''

''Yes, of course. But he didn't believe me. He said he was following up on confidential information he'd received from my husband.'' She fought for control, her fury at the unconscionable slur threatening to cause another feminine release. ''He claimed you'd been indiscreet during a recent phone conversation.''

''I haven't spoken to a reporter in over a year.''

She waved that aside, the brandy swirling in her glass.
"I know it wasn't you. I'm sure it must have been
Cornell. Though how he got hold of Loren's medical
records I can't begin to guess."

"Can't you?" Stefano poured himself a whiskey and
turned to face her. "I hate to say this, but your uncle's
condition has deteriorated noticeably these past few
months. You said so yourself. A good investigator could
have uncovered the information for Cornell." He took a
long swallow of his drink. "No doubt this is the wedding
present he promised."

She started. "Of course. He promised to deliver it as
soon as we tied the knot."

"Hang in there, sweetheart," Stefano reassured.
"We'll figure a way out of this mess."

"I waited too long before marrying, didn't I?" She
leaned her head back against the couch cushions and
closed her eyes. "The value of Crabbe is plummeting as
we speak and it's all my fault. I've done what damage
control I could, but it won't be enough."

"This isn't your fault," Stefano announced grimly.
"It's mine. I shouldn't have challenged Cornell."

That caught her by surprise. She took another sip of
brandy and regarded her husband over the rim of the
glass. How chivalrous of him to take responsibility. And
how typical. "It isn't your fault. You haven't done anything wrong. And one of these days—no matter what it
takes—I'm going to prove it."

"That's my sweet, logical, unemotional wife." He
joined her on the couch, pulling her into his arms.
"Don't worry, *cara*. You have all the Salvatores behind
you. And you'll find we're a determined bunch."

She relaxed against his shoulder. "There's one bright
spot."

"What is it?"

"My lawyer received an offer to purchase Crabbe late yesterday. Even after they heard today's news, they didn't back out."

"A lowball offer?" he asked neutrally.

"How'd you know?"

"Lucky guess."

"If I can get some concessions for the staff, I might accept it."

"Who made the offer?"

Her brow wrinkled in concentration. "A firm called Obit. Ever heard of them?"

"Doesn't ring any bells."

"The amount they've proposed would be ridiculous under normal circumstances, but combined with what I received from you for Janus, it should be enough to take care of Loren."

He brushed a lock of hair from her face, the gesture unexpectedly intimate. "What about taking care of you?"

"I'm used to working for my living." She laughed, the sound empty of humor. "Though I doubt anyone will hire an executive officer who managed to ruin her family's business the minute she got her hands on it. Do you?"

"I already told you. This isn't your fault."

"Maybe not. But it's my responsibility."

Stefano sighed. "I apologize, Nellie. I promised to protect you and I've let you down. I knew Cornell would make good on his threat. But instead of going after him and finding out what he planned, I waited."

"You couldn't have known he'd do this."

"Maybe not." Stefano's mouth tightened. "But he's made one mistake. A big one."

"And what mistake is that?"

"No one harms what belongs to me. He'll pay for what he's done. I'll see to it personally."

She stirred uneasily. "I don't belong to you."

"Don't you?" His dark eyes gleamed with amusement. "After what happened last night, after all that was said between us this morning, you can still think that? Do you even realize that you almost knocked Marco over trying to get to me a few minutes ago? There's only one explanation for that. You *know*. You feel the difference between us now. You and I belong to each other."

He'd alarmed her again, just as he had this morning. "How many times do I have to say it? Our marriage is not real," she retaliated. "In fact, if this new offer works out and I sell Crabbe and Associates, we won't need to maintain even that fiction."

"Our marriage is not fiction." His accent was stronger than she'd ever heard it, underscoring his fury. "The vows we spoke were sacred."

She pulled free of his arms, determined to put some distance between them. "They were also supposed to be temporary. We agreed to that."

"And what about the other promise you made? Or will that be broken, as well?"

"If you're referring to restoring your reputation, we don't have to be married to accomplish that."

Without a word, he stood and crossed the room to stand by the windows. Light surrounded him like a halo, flashing in the darkness of his hair and emphasizing the intense pitch-black of his suit. Very gently he set his empty whiskey tumbler on his desk, then turned to face her. His features were thrown into shadow, making it impossible to read his expression.

"It's clear you've thought this through. What are your plans, Penelope?"

She froze. He'd called her Penelope again. It was only the second time he'd ever done that. She fought a rush of dread. Why should she be so worried? She wasn't attached to Stefano. Not really. They shared an enjoyable physical relationship and that was all. If they parted, she'd regret it, but life would continue.

Wouldn't it?

"I'm going to schedule a meeting with Obit and see if selling Crabbe is feasible," she informed her husband.

"And then?"

"Stefano, please. We don't need to decide this now."

"I think we do." He folded his arms across his chest. "What happens after you've sold out."

She flinched at his phrasing. "Then I'll do everything I can to prove your innocence."

"What about us?"

"We'll..." She moistened her lips. "We'll do the sensible thing. We'll separate."

"Very logical."

"I warned you I was," she said, desperation creeping into her voice. "This can't come as a surprise to you."

He shook his head, the movement infinitely weary. "You've picked the damnedest time to start acting logical, my love. I just hope you don't regret your choice." He crossed to his office door and opened it. It was clear their discussion was over. "Call me when you've scheduled the meeting with Obit."

She stood, startled to discover that her legs were reluctant to support her. "You want to attend?"

"Not only do I want to attend, but I also want your assurance that you won't conduct the meeting without me by your side." He waited until she'd drawn level to him before sliding a hand across her cheek. "Do this one thing for me and I won't ask for anymore."

She inclined her head in agreement. "All right. I'll let you know as soon as the arrangements have been made."

The open doorway yawned before her. She glanced at Stefano. Always before he'd kissed her whenever they'd parted. A part of her longed for that kiss, but one look warned it wasn't to come. Setting her chin, she forced herself to walk out the door.

"One more thing, Mrs. Salvatore."

She swung around with embarrassing eagerness. "Yes?"

"About that other promise. I wasn't referring to your restoring my reputation. I was referring to a promise you made last night." His gaze held hers, fierce with determination. "It's a promise I intend to hold you to."

Stefano stood at his office window and stared across the street toward Crabbe and Associates. Dammit all! He slammed his fist against the shatter-proof glass. He'd pushed too hard, too soon, forcing emotions on her that she wasn't ready to accept. He'd also forced her to confront her own emotions, something she *really* wasn't ready to accept. And as a result his darling wife had flat-out panicked. Worse, she'd turned tail and run.

He'd thought after they'd made love that she'd face the truth, that the bond between them would break through her fear. That she'd realize that her emotions weren't something to avoid, but to embrace. For one brief moment, she'd done just that. And then morning had come and she'd launched a full-scale retreat.

The irony drove him insane. Everything she did, every decision she made came from the passionate core within her. Not that she could see that. She'd spent too many years believing herself cool, analytical and logical. But she wasn't. She was a woman made for love. His love. All he had to do was prove that to her.

Stefano splayed his hand over the glass and stared hungrily across the street.

Come back to me, Nellie. I love you.

Penelope stood at her office window and stared across the street toward Salvatores. Darn it! She leaned her forehead against the shatter-proof glass. She'd sure handled that brilliantly, hadn't she? He'd pushed too hard, too soon, forcing emotions on her that she wasn't ready to accept and she'd panicked. Worse, she'd turned tail and run. And all because he'd made such a big deal about her newfound ability to tell him from Marco.

So they'd made love. And right after that she'd known—with a visceral certainty—which of the two men was her husband. Well, what did he expect? It was bound to happen eventually. It didn't mean they'd forged any sort of mystical, emotional connection. Did it? The whole incident was perfectly logical, attributable to her analytical skills and deductive reasoning.

Plus the fact that she loved him.

Penelope fought to breathe, to think, to acknowledge any sort of sensory input other than that one startling discovery. Staring in disbelief, she stepped back from the window. After all her fiery denials, after all her talk of lust over love, somehow she'd done the unthinkable—she'd allowed her heart to overrule her head.

She loved him!

The more she thought about it, the more positive she became. Just repeating the words brought with them a bone-deep certainty, a rightness, such as when she evaluated a problem and deduced the perfect solution. Or when she negotiated a contract and all the pieces came together in a perfect whole. How could she have been so blind? It was so obvious. So logical. So eminently rational. It made perfect sense, considering Stefano's charm and grace and integrity. It would have been strange if she hadn't fallen in love with him. Nor could she have given herself to him if she hadn't been in love.

Relief surged through her. She didn't need to be afraid or shy away from emotions that were so reasonable. Stefano was an honorable man. He'd never hurt her. He'd promised to protect her and that meant he'd even protect her from himself. If he said he loved her then she could trust him to love her for all the days of her life. She nibbled on her lower lip. Now she faced one small problem. How did she fix what had gone so terribly wrong between them? After the way they'd parted, how in the world did she tell him that she'd suddenly discovered she loved him?

And then she remembered her wedding night promise—and that he planned to hold her to that promise. A lopsided grin broke across her face and she stared out the window with renewed determination. There was one thing she could do. She could get rid of Crabbe. And maybe she could even get the facts necessary to restore his reputation. With those goals accomplished there wouldn't be anything else standing between them, at least no business reasons for their marriage to continue. Then she'd have a chance of convincing him that she loved him and only him.

Penelope splayed her hand over the glass and stared hungrily across the street.

Hang on, my love. I'm coming.

CHAPTER TEN

"READY?" Stefano asked.

Penelope nodded. "As ready as I'll ever be." She hesitated, aware that it was much too soon to say anything about her recent discovery, but unable to help herself. "After this is over, we need to talk."

"You're damned right," her husband concurred in a grim voice.

Cindy peeked into the conference room. "The people from Obit are here. Shall I send them in?"

Penelope nodded. "Yes, please." The sooner the better.

"Prepare yourself," Stefano muttered.

Before she could ask what he meant, a man stepped over the threshold—the last man she'd expected or ever wanted to see. Robert Cornell.

He smiled expansively at them. "Why, hello, Penelope, Salvatore. I did warn we'd meet again."

Years of practice came to her rescue. She didn't miss a beat, but accepted his comment with calm acknowledgment. "So you did. I shouldn't be surprised to see you here. But I am."

"Your husband isn't."

She turned and looked at Stefano, registering the truth for herself. A hint of vulnerability betrayed her before she could suppress it. "Cornell's right. You're not surprised, are you?"

"No," Stefano admitted.

She started to speak, then broke off, switching her

attention back to Cornell. "Excuse us, won't you? My husband and I need to confer."

"I suspected you might." He took a seat at the head of the table and made himself comfortable, eyeing the room with a proprietary air. "Don't take too long, though. I'm not a patient man."

Head held high, Penelope led the way from the conference room to her office. Once there she turned on him. "How could you? You knew Cornell was behind the offer, didn't you?"

"I suspected."

"Why didn't you warn me?"

"Because I couldn't prove anything." He smiled dryly. "Cornell is a tough man to pin down. You should know that by now. I could have been wrong and I didn't see any point in getting you upset over something that might not happen. Now that the worse has been confirmed, we can deal with it."

"I won't sell to him!"

"I was hoping you'd say that. In fact, you don't have to sell at all."

She paced the length of the room. "I should allow Crabbe to go bankrupt instead?"

"Bankruptcy is not the inevitable outcome, Nellie," he argued. "You're part of the Salvatore family now. We can help you hold Crabbe together until you're ready to take over or until the business is rebuilt enough to market for something approaching its true value."

A frown formed between her brows. This wasn't what she'd planned. She wanted to end all business ties between them, not create more. "But what about your reputation? If you and your brothers step in to help, people will say you deliberately released the information about Loren so you could take control of my firm."

He shrugged. "It's already being said. Time should put an end to the speculation."

"Not if Cornell keeps spreading rumors. And not if he finds another way to get at us."

"With luck he'll grow bored and turn his attention elsewhere."

She regarded him with a skeptical expression. "He won't give up if he's as vindictive as you believe."

"Come on, Nellie. Don't let him take your company." Stefano held out his hand. "Let's throw him out together."

Before she could respond, Cindy walked in. "Excuse me, Mrs. Salvatore. I have papers related to the sale ready for you to sign. Shall I notify your lawyer to come in?"

Penelope hesitated. "If I sell to Cornell, he gets everything," she said, working it through aloud. "If I don't sell to him, I risk bankruptcy and he still accomplishes his goal. Either way, your reputation is in shreds."

"To hell with my reputation! What happens to me isn't the issue."

"It *is* the issue to me." She reached a decision. "No. I can't walk away. Not until I force Cornell to admit the truth. Chances are good that I'm going down. There's not much I can do about that. But I can still help you."

"Dammit, Nellie." He thrust his hand through his hair, annoyance glittering in his dark gaze. "Why doesn't it surprise me that you'd end up making this choice, particularly considering it's the least reasonable of all your options? Please, *cara*. Be sensible. Trying to salvage my reputation isn't worth losing Crabbe over."

She brushed that aside. "Don't be ridiculous. I never do anything unless it's both reasonable and sensible."

She switched her attention to her assistant. "Cindy, get the papers."

"Your lawyer has asked to be present when you sign."

"Then send him in."

Mr. Wilfred entered the room a moment later. He nodded at Stefano and took up a stance by Penelope's desk. "You're certain you want to give up your rights, Mrs. Salvatore?"

"Quite certain."

"Please read the papers before signing," he instructed.

"No need. I read everything earlier."

"Mrs. Salvatore, I strongly urge—"

She cut him off impatiently. "There's no time, Mr. Wilfred. I promise you. I did read them very carefully earlier."

Cindy placed a thick stack of papers on Penelope's desk and handed over a pen. She ruffled through the contract and pointed. "Sign here and here."

"Nellie—" Stefano began again.

"I have a plan," she interrupted, hastily scratching her signature across the pages. "I think we can salvage the situation. But you have to trust me."

He removed his suit jacket and tossed it over the back of a nearby chair. Approaching the desk, he rested his hip on the corner. "I trust you with my life. You must know that by now."

Penelope paused long enough to smile up at him. She'd been so foolish running from her feelings for Stefano. He meant everything to her. And shortly she'd prove it. "I do know you trust me. And I appreciate it very much."

"Do you also trust me?" he asked.

She didn't hesitate. "Of course. But that doesn't have anything to do with my plan."

"What plan?"

"Sign here, Mrs. Salvatore," Cindy interrupted. "And then initial each page."

Penelope obediently applied herself to the task while continuing to address Stefano. "I think I can get Cornell to confess to what he's done."

He caught her hand and drew it away from the contract. "How?"

"Let me get these signed and I'll tell you."

"Nellie, you're moving too fast. Tell me your idea first. Then if you're still determined, you can sign the papers."

A glimmer of amusement lit her face. "You mean if you don't succeed in talking me out of it first?"

His mouth twitched. "That, too."

She put down her pen. "Okay. Here's the plan. Our boardroom has a video camera tucked away in one corner. Very unobtrusive. You wouldn't even see it unless you knew to look there. We use it during our meetings to make a record of our discussions in case any questions arise later. I'm going to have Cindy activate the camera. Then I'm going to get Cornell to confess before selling Crabbe and Associates."

"And if he won't?"

"We'll just have to make sure he does." She signed the last of the pages and shoved the documents across the desk to Cindy. "I made a promise to you, Stefano. I told you I'd restore your honor and that's precisely what I intend to do."

Stefano glanced at the lawyer and Cindy, jerking his head toward the office door. They took the hint and left. The minute he was alone with his wife, he gathered her into his arms. "Don't you understand? You restored my honor weeks ago. You did that when you walked into my office and proposed. You were the only one outside of the family who believed in my innocence. And you've continued to believe even when all the evidence indicated I was guilty."

She smiled up at him. "I explained all that. It was simple logic. I reviewed all the information, examined the various facts and reached a conclusion based on the evidence at hand."

He lowered his head, his mouth a breath away from hers. "*Cara mia,*" he whispered. "How many times do *I* have to tell *you*? The evidence condemned me."

She closed the tiny gap separating them and kissed him...kissed him with a hunger he couldn't mistake, telling him without words how she felt. "The conclusions drawn from that evidence were flawed. It just needed someone impartial to review the case."

"You're not going to admit to bias, are you?"

"Bias in favor of my husband? Don't be ridiculous." Her amusement faded, replaced by impassioned resolve. "You're an honorable man, Mr. Salvatore. And anyone who says different will have to deal with me."

"I was once a man of honor," he told her regretfully. "Now I'm a man who will do anything and everything to protect his wife."

She stared in confusion. Now what in the world did that mean? "I don't need protection."

He didn't bother arguing. "What do you need?" he asked instead.

"This..."

Her mouth returned to his, forging a delicious union. For the first time since she'd mentioned a separation, he felt a resurgence of hope. She couldn't kiss him like this, respond to him like this if she wanted their marriage to end. She sank into the embrace with a soft moan, her hands fluttering from his shoulders to his chest. Giving in to the inevitable, he allowed her to strip away his tie and unbutton his shirt. As much as he'd like to wrinkle her a little in return, he didn't dare. If she was going to confront Cornell, she'd need all the self-confidence at her disposal.

It wasn't until she encountered his bare chest that she came to her senses and reluctantly pulled away. "Stefano?"

"Yes, *cara?*"

"I have a confession."

"And that would be?"

She hesitated. "Maybe it should wait until after we've dealt with Cornell."

He shook his head. "No, Nellie. Make your confession now. That way you won't be able to change your mind if things don't go as planned."

"Okay." She moistened her lips. "I may have been hasty in suggesting we separate."

He smiled tenderly. "An excellent confession, sweetheart."

"I've been thinking." Her brows drew together. "If I leave you now, it could hurt your reputation."

He swore beneath his breath in virulent Italian. "Dammit, Nellie! Not this again."

She halted the barrage of words with her fingertips. "No, listen. If I sell Crabbe and then leave you, people will say it's because you didn't get what you wanted. If we beat Cornell and I leave, they'll think I uncovered something that discredited you. Either way, you'll pay the ultimate price."

"Do you think I give a damn about any of that?"

"No. But I do. Our marriage was my idea. You were supposed to benefit from it, not be hurt."

"You could never hurt me."

Her mouth trembled for a brief instant before she firmed it. "I already have. And I'm more sorry than I can possibly say."

Stefano couldn't decide whether to laugh or grab Penelope and try to kiss some sense into her. Her confession wasn't what he wanted to hear. He'd hoped for a vow of undying love. He'd expected to hear her admit that she'd been wrong and that their marriage was a love affair that would endure for the rest of their lives. His hands collapsed into fists. As soon as he'd taken care of Cornell, he'd have to explain to Penelope how this wife business worked. Explain it in clear, rational, logical terms so his dear, sweet, overly emotional bride would understand.

"Thank you for your confession," he muttered. "I think. Are you ready to take care of Cornell now?"

"As ready as I'll ever be."

She rubbed a trace of lipstick from his mouth and applied herself to his buttons, before straightening his tie. As soon as she'd finished, he slipped on his suit jacket and searched through his pockets for his tie clasp. He glanced at his wife, watching as she checked her makeup and hair. Satisfied, she faced him, offering a brilliant smile filled with grace and sweetness and unmistakable love. Did she even realize how she felt about him? Unlikely, considering how hard she fought the mere suggestion of emotional involvement.

"Nice tie tack," she chattered, her nervousness getting the better of her. "Very fancy. It doesn't have your name on it like the one I gave you, but it'll do."

"A recent purchase." He wrapped an arm around her shoulders. "Come on. Let's go."

"Wait. There's one more thing I forgot to mention."

He released his breath in a long-suffering sigh. "Another confession?"

"Yes, another one."

"Go ahead." He folded his arms across his chest. "You might as well get them all out in the open."

"Okay. I love you." With a brisk nod, she headed for the door. Once there, she hesitated. "Ready?"

"Cara?"

She regarded him uncertainly. "Yes?"

It took every ounce of self-control to keep from sweeping her into his arms and carrying her right out of the building. *She loved him!* He allowed himself a quick, triumphant grin. "Your timing leaves something to be desired."

"Yes, it often does," she admitted regretfully. "I'm afraid that's what happens when you have a logical bent of mind. It can take a while to work through all the variables and arrive at an accurate conclusion."

The urge to kiss her was replaced by a far different urge. He promised himself he'd have ample opportunity to express his objection to her 'logical bent' soon enough. "You realize we'll have to discuss this later."

Her mouth tilted into a wry smile. "I assumed as much. Stefano?"

"Yes, love?"

"Are you very angry?"

"Very." He relented ever so slightly. "But I expect I'll get over it."

Cornell was waiting impatiently for their return, his lawyer standing protectively behind him. "Well? What's the decision?"

"We'll sell," Penelope announced. "But on one condition."

His expression grew cynical. "There's always a condition."

"Let's see whether you're willing to agree to this one. Because, I assure you, it's a deal breaker if you don't."

"Go on."

"I want the truth about what happened with the Bennetts."

"You're joking."

"Not even a little."

"What makes you think I have information about that deal?" Cornell glanced at Stefano. "Perhaps you should ask your husband since he was the one directly involved."

"Cut the crap, Cornell," Stefano interrupted. "We're not asking you to make a public announcement. We simply require confirmation from you."

"Just out of curiosity, what will you do with that confirmation?"

Stefano shoved his hands into his pockets. "There's not much we can do, is there?"

"Then why bother?"

Time to let a bit of air out of the man's overinflated ego. "I want to know once and for all whether you really are clever enough to pull off the perfect scam. You'll excuse me if I confess to having doubts."

"What you really mean is... Was it a lucky coincidence on my part or actual skill. Yes, I can see where the curiosity must be killing you. Okay, I'll throw you a bone. I'll tell you what I know about the Bennett situation." His voice flattened, acquiring an implacable tone. "But not until *after* Mrs. Salvatore signs the papers."

Stefano shook his head. "Not a chance."

"What's wrong?" Cornell mocked. "Don't you trust me?"

"Not even a little."

"Then it would appear we're at a stalemate."

"I'll agree to signing first," Penelope spoke up. "If you'll agree to my lawyer holding the contract—without your signature—until after we've heard the truth."

Stefano wished his wife wouldn't prove herself so damned predictable. "Don't, Nellie! This isn't what we discussed. It's not worth the—"

She cut him off. "Don't worry, Stefano. I know what I'm doing."

"That's open to debate."

Cornell held up his hand. "You sign and *my* lawyer will hold the documents," he countered. "Salvatore can always tackle him and snatch the contract back if I don't live up to my end of the bargain."

"Fine," Penelope concurred. "Your lawyer. Then once you've given us what we want, Crabbe is officially turned over to you and you can leave."

"We'll conduct our…discussion in private?" Cornell interrupted, sensing victory.

"Of course."

"Don't do it, Nellie," Stefano attempted to reason with her. "Not for my sake. The price is too high."

Cornell rubbed his hands together. "I believe we have a deal."

"Sir," Cornell's lawyer interrupted. "I must agree with Mr. Salvatore. This is not advisable. I most strongly recommend you—"

"As the lady said, we know what we're doing, Curtis."

"Sir—"

Cornell's good humor vanished. "Bring everyone in here and let's get the final papers signed before Salvatore—or my own damned lawyer—convinces Mrs. Salvatore to change her mind."

It didn't take long for all the lawyers and assistants to crowd into the room. In short order, Penelope had affixed her signature to the remaining documents. "I thought I took care of most of these earlier," she muttered at one point.

"Just keep signing," Wilfred instructed. "Unless you've changed your mind?"

"Don't sound so hopeful." The minute she'd finished, she handed the documents to Curtis. "Clear the room, please. Mr. Cornell and I have some unfinished business to discuss."

The instant the three of them were alone, she turned to Cornell. "Well? I believe you have something to tell us. And let me warn you, if I don't hear the truth about who defrauded the Bennetts, I'll tear up those documents myself."

Cornell stood and stretched. "Oh, you'll have the truth. Just one brief delay before we get down to business." Shoving a chair to the corner of the room, he positioned it beneath the video camera mounted near the ceiling. Standing on the seat, he ripped out the wiring. He threw Penelope a mocking smile over his shoulder. "I almost didn't see this. It's well disguised. But I trust you'll understand that I don't intend to have any recordings of my confession."

Every scrap of color bleached from Penelope's cheeks and Stefano crossed to her side, dropping his hands on her shoulders. "Easy," he murmured.

Cornell clicked his tongue in admonishment. "You didn't really think I was so gullible, did you? There could only be one reason why you'd want my confession in exchange for Crabbe and Associates. I kept looking until I found it.''

She tilted her chin to a defiant angle. ''Does that mean you're going to break the deal?''

''Not at all. I've disabled your camera. There's no reason not to finalize our agreement.''

''Are you sure you don't want to search us in case we're bugged?'' she asked bitterly.

''Not necessary, my dear. Your reaction when I disabled your precious camera tells me you only had the one card to play.'' He thrust the chair back toward the table and resumed his seat. ''You know, my lawyer's right. This isn't a smart move on my part. It's never wise to confess one's crimes.''

''Then why do it?'' she questioned.

''Because he can't resist,'' Stefano replied. ''His ego demands it. He doesn't want us to have the least doubt that he outmaneuvered us on each and every front, starting with the Bennetts.''

''Wrong again, Salvatore. It didn't start with the Bennetts.'' He aimed a cold gaze toward Penelope. ''It started with Janus Corp. Unfortunately that didn't last long because your wife destroyed a particularly sweet deal I had going there.''

Penelope's mouth dropped open. *''What?''*

''Come now, Mrs. Salvatore. Don't look so shocked. I couldn't very well use my own company as a front for a smuggling operation. What if I'd been caught? No, far better that some other enterprise take the risks for me.'' He smiled expansively. ''You know, it's such a pleasure to have the two of you together like this. I can't tell you how much satisfaction it gives me to watch you both fall and fall hard. Two birds with one stone. A trite little cliché, but true nonetheless.''

"You…you were the one who used Janus Corp to smuggle black market items?'' Penelope asked in disbelief. "And you were behind the dummy corporation that took the Bennetts' money, as well?''

Cornell sighed. "Guilty as charged.''

"And putting the blame on Stefano. That was you, too?''

"Guilty and guiltier.''

"What about spreading the rumors about Loren Wentworth?'' Stefano inserted smoothly, giving Penelope's shoulders another warning squeeze. "I assume that was also your work?''

"I felt a certain responsibility to alert people that the head of Crabbe and Associates wasn't competent.''

"Regardless of the report's veracity?''

Cornell lifted an eyebrow. "It's not true?'' He shrugged. "Oh, well. The rumor accomplished what I'd intended, which is all that matters. The value of the company took a nosedive enabling me to pick it up at a rock-bottom price. Calling *Financial News* and posing as you, Salvatore, was a particular stroke of genius, don't you think?''

"I assume you used my name to create doubt in Nellie's mind about me?'' Stefano continued.

"Not that it worked,'' Cornell replied. "For a reasonably intelligent woman, she seems quite irrational where you're concerned.''

"Irrational!''

"Easy, *cara.*''

"I'm not the least irrational.'' She glared at her nemesis. "I'll have you know that I'm one of the most logical, analytical—''

Cornell waved her silent. "Are we through here? I'd like to leave."

"Oh, we're through," Stefano assured. "There's just one problem."

"And what's that?"

"I'm afraid you'll find you paid a lot of money for very little."

"Good try, Salvatore. But I don't consider Crabbe and Associates a 'little' company."

"It isn't. It's my wife's interest in the company that's small. And that's what you bought. Her interest. As of thirty minutes ago she owned precisely one percent of the entire company. Now, if she'd decided to sell you Salvatores, you could have made out quite well. She owns approximately ninety-nine percent of that company."

Penelope turned to stare at him, her mouth dropping open again. "What?"

"The papers you just signed. We traded ownership." Stefano's gaze fixed on Cornell and he offered a cold smile. "You know how it is with married couples. What's hers is mine. What's mine is hers."

"This won't hold up in a court of law! It's fraud."

"Somehow I don't think this will ever come to court. I think you'll have other legal matters occupying your attention." He raised his voice. "Did you get Cornell's confession, Wilfred?"

The door popped open. "It came through just fine, Mr. Salvatore. I'm afraid we had to physically restrain Mr. Curtis. He was most unhappy with the direction of your conversation. The newspaper people were quite intrigued, though. I believe they'd like to ask Mr. Cornell some questions."

Tears formed in Penelope's eyes. "How? When? I don't understand any of this."

"Let's send Cornell on his way and then I'll answer all your questions." Removing his tie clip and the miniaturized audio/video equipment, Stefano deactivated everything and tossed the pieces to the conference table. "I think we're done with these. Especially since I'd rather not record the rest of our conversation."

Cornell leapt to his feet, his hands bunching into fists. "You'll pay for what you've done, Salvatore."

Stefano simply shrugged. "Since you appreciate trite little clichés, how about this one? In for a penny…" He dropped Cornell with a single powerful, eminently satisfying blow. "In for a pound."

Penelope came to stand beside him, her golden eyes reflecting her approval. "I wonder if Don Quixote ever tried doing things your way, Stefano. I'll bet he'd have defeated some of those windmills if he had."

"Or maybe we should change that bronze statue you bought me from Quixote to Rocky Balboa." Stefano returned his attention to the man draped across his wife's conference room floor. "Listen up, Cornell. The Bennetts didn't deserve what you did to them. Nor did my wife. Touch either of them again and you won't have one Salvatore to deal with, you'll have six."

"That's right," Penelope contributed. "Nobody messes with what belongs to my husband. I hope you've learned your lesson."

Opening the door to the conference room, Stefano picked Cornell up by his lapels and thrust him from the room. "He's all yours," he called to the newspeople. "Thanks for loaning me the surveillance equipment. And Cindy? Bring in the documents my wife signed earlier. All of them."

Then he turned to face his wife. The remains of her tears were still evident, glistening on the ends of her lashes. But her mouth had lost its tremulous set. He regarded her warily, not quite certain how she was going to react, particularly since he'd broken the terms of their marriage agreement by not checking with her before acting. Perhaps this would be a good time to renegotiate.

"I assume you'd like an explanation," he said.

"If it wouldn't be too much trouble. I gather I'm no longer the owner of Crabbe and Associates?"

He shrugged. "You wouldn't have been, anyway. Not if you'd given Cornell what he wanted. As soon as everything calms down, Wilfred has papers that will set matters right and transfer ownership again. Plus, no one will believe the rumors about Loren now that they know Cornell was responsible for spreading them. It should help boost the value of Crabbe."

"Why didn't you tell me?"

Hurt riddled her voice and he winced. He'd known she wouldn't take this well. "Because Cornell would have guessed something was up. He believed he was safe because *you* believed it."

She glanced toward the equipment on the conference table. "You were wired. How could I have missed that when I kissed you?"

"I put it on later, while you were fixing your makeup. You were too distracted to notice." He shot her a speaking look. "I have to admit, I had a few heart-stopping moments there when you suggested he search us."

His comment won him a brief smile. "How could you be sure Cornell would tell us the truth?"

"I couldn't. I took a risk. Even if it had backfired, he wouldn't have benefited. You didn't own more than one percent of Crabbe, remember? He would have torn those documents up himself rather than pay the agreed upon price for such a paltry share of the company.'' Stefano grimaced. ''Of course, then he would have sued us. But I hoped it wouldn't come to that.''

A knock sounded at the door and Cindy entered. She dropped a stack of papers on the table and then quickly left. Penelope fingered the contracts, though she didn't make any move to examine them. ''You...'' She moistened her lips. ''If the deal had gone wrong you would have destroyed your reputation beyond any hope of redemption. You sacrificed everything for my sake.''

''If I sacrificed everything, so did you. The only way those papers transferring ownership would have been signed was if you'd decided to do something foolishly noble, like try to salvage my reputation by selling Crabbe to Cornell at a huge loss. If you'd refused to sell, those contracts would never have seen the light of day. And as long as we're discussing compromising our values, what about you?''

''Me?'' Her head jerked up. ''What are you talking about?''

He started toward her. ''I'm talking about you, Ms. Logic-at-all-costs. You made a business decision based on pure emotion. Admit it.''

She folded her arms across her chest. ''I'm not going to admit any such thing. I considered my options and chose the most reasonable one available to me.''

''You gave away your company for peanuts so you could try to restore my reputation. I don't call that reasonable.'' He halted inches away. ''It would seem we have a problem, Mrs. Salvatore.''

''And what's that?''

''When you signed those papers you became the new owner of Salvatores.''

She picked up the pertinent contract and paged through it. The paper trembled in her hand. "All of you signed it."

"Every last Salvatore. We had to. It wouldn't have been legal otherwise."

"But your brothers all agreed to it. Even your father did. Why would they do that? It doesn't make a bit of sense." He could hear the plea in her voice. "I don't understand."

"Don't you?" He took the contract from her hand and tossed it to the table. The pages spilled across the gleaming wood surface, scattering. "You're family."

"But our marriage… They thought it would be temporary."

"No." He caught her close. "They knew it wouldn't be. I suspect you're the only one who believed our marriage was an actual business proposition. It's turned out to be more than that, hasn't it?"

Her breath shuddered in her lungs. "Are you suggesting we make it permanent?"

He smiled tenderly. "It already is, *cara.* It became real the minute you spoke your vows. You proved that when you shared my bed. You proved it again when you shoved past Marco to get to me. And you proved it today, by trying to salvage my reputation, even if it meant sacrificing Crabbe and Associates."

"Oh, that. It was a—"

"*Please.* Don't tell me that was a reasonable decision."

"But it was. A reasonable decision based on careful analytical deduction." A frown creased her brow. "Though now that I think about it, your own deductive skills must be quite impressive. In order for you to set all this up, you had to know how I'd react each step of the way.''

''It was a struggle.''

''Sarcasm, Stefano?''

''Not even a little. Admiration, Mrs. Salvatore. You are the most generous woman I've ever met. Given that, I just had to determine all the possible scenarios and decide which choices a woman in love would make.'' He paused a beat before continuing. ''Because you are in love with me, aren't you?''

The tears returned, unchecked. ''You know I am. I told you this morning, as well as last night. I also made you a promise when we made love.''

He closed his eyes for a brief moment. ''You *do* remember. I wondered.''

''I believe my exact words were that I'd love you to the end of all time.'' She smiled through her tears. ''I was feeling unusually poetic, perhaps because of what we were doing.''

''I love you, Nellie. And I particularly love you when you're feeling unusually poetic.'' He cupped her face. ''I think I fell for you the minute you marched into my office and offered yourself to me.''

''I didn't offer myself,'' she corrected. ''I offered you a business deal.''

''A deal I couldn't resist. In fact, falling in love with you was the most logical choice I could make.''

She nodded approvingly. ''I knew you'd see things my way. Logic before emotion. It's the only way.''

''*Nellie!*''

''You might as well get used to it,'' she informed him airily. ''You're an excessively emotional man and you've chosen to marry a woman your exact opposite.

It's not going to be easy for you to deal with my logical turn of mind.''

"Oh, no?" he growled. His hands slipped into her hair and he tilted her face up to his. "I can think of one way." And then he proved it in a most reasonable and logical—if excessively emotional—manner possible.

He kissed her until she'd stripped them both naked.

MAITLAND MATERNITY

Where the luckiest babies are born!

Join Harlequin® and Silhouette® for a special 12-book series about the world-renowned Maitland Maternity Clinic, owned and operated by the prominent Maitland family of Austin, Texas, where romances are born, secrets are revealed...and bundles of joy are delivered!

Look for

MAITLAND MATERNITY

titles at your favorite retail outlet, starting in August 2000

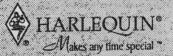
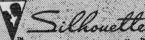

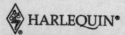

HARLEQUIN®

Harlequin Romance®

Coming Next Month

#3615 BACHELOR IN NEED Jessica Steele
Jegar Urquart needed Fennia's help in looking after his niece while
her parents were in hospital. Jegar clearly found Fennia attractive...
but while she could answer Jegar's need for a live-in nanny, Fennia
felt she must resist slipping into the role of live-in lover as well!

The Marriage Pledge

#3616 A MOTHER FOR MOLLIE Barbara McMahon
Patrick O'Shaunnessy can't help Shelby unravel her past—he's too
busy trying to run his investigative business and care for his little
girl! So Shelby suggests a temporary marriage: she'll look after his
daughter while he works for her. But Shelby starts wanting a more
permanent arrangement....

Beaufort Brides

#3617 THE FAITHFUL BRIDE Rebecca Winters
Years after Wade had called off their wedding, Janet found out why:
a friend had told him she was having an affair! Now Janet wanted
another wedding. She knew Wade would have no doubt of her
innocence come the honeymoon! But first she had to convince
him she was a bride worth trusting....

White Weddings

#3618 HIS DESERT ROSE Liz Fielding
When Prince Hassan al Rashid drew the world's media attention to
the abduction of well-known foreign correspondent Rose Fenton,
he also lost his heart. And, kidnapped by Hassan, Rose was
surprised to find that beneath the designer suit lay the heart of a
true desert prince!

CNM0700